The Paris Footman

A Regency Romance

Rosanne E. Lortz

MADISON STREET
PUBLISHING

preux chevalier

a white knight, a Sir Galahad
a man of courtesy and chivalry to all the fairer sex

Prologue

LONDON, ENGLAND ~ JUNE 1806

LADY LOUISA SAT ON a stone bench in the garden behind Carlton House and folded her hands neatly in her lap. *Back straight, chin up!*

Louisa adjusted her posture to allow her white muslin skirts to fall gracefully about her ankles and adopted a poise of sophistication beyond her sixteen years. If she pretended that she was supremely indifferent to her solitary situation, perhaps no one would be any the wiser.

On a whim, her father, the Duke of Warrenton, had brought her with him to Prince George's residence that afternoon, assuming that she could amuse the eleven-year-old Princess Charlotte. But then—when he had seen that Princess Charlotte was not in attendance and had observed the rackety set of *roués* who were—he had sent her outside to sit in the garden while he stayed inside the royal mansion to finish up his cognac and conversations. Louisa sighed. It was six o'clock already, she had missed tea, and she suspected that her father might have overindulged in a stronger drink and forgotten about her altogether.

She hoped that her father had not been distracted by something in the petticoat line. *That* was always a fear where the Duke of Warrenton was concerned. Thankfully, Louisa's sharp eyes had noted that there were only a few ladies inside the great house. One of them, whom her father had addressed as Lady Hertford, seemed to be the unquestioned queen bee of the bunch, but the fat fellow whom Louisa recognised as Prince George was hovering around her like a bear by a honey tree. She could tell from the way he touched Lady Hertford's arm and leaned in towards her rouged cheek that she was *his* mistress. At least Louisa was safe from seeing her father coquetting in that direction.

She ought to have been unaware of such liaisons. Most sixteen-year-old girls of good breeding would have been. But then, Louisa had been raised in a rackety household herself. Her flighty French mother, the former Comtesse Dammartin, had died when she was only eight, and she had been left for indifferent servants to mind as the duke gadded about from hunting lodge to horse race to house party. Throughout her adolescent years, her father had materialised at infrequent intervals like an Arabian djinn—neglectful, but then regretful; austere, but then ostentatious with his largesse.

This "treat" of bringing her to Carlton House and then shuffling her off to the gardens was just another example of his mercurial nature. How self-indulgent of him to assume that his own amusements would be equally amusing to a girl of sixteen. How typical of him to forget her existence as soon as the prince ushered him into the inner circle. No doubt this was how he had treated his younger brother, Uncle Nigel, all his life—as an entity to be considered only when completely convenient. No doubt this was how he had treated Louisa's mother, until the two of them led such separate lives that her father had barely mourned when her mother passed away from a sudden pneumonia.

Idiot girl! Take yourself home in the carriage.

The Warrenton coachman would be obliged to take her home if she asked him. But she kept hoping—against past experience—that her father would join her within the next quarter hour, making it unnecessary for her to depart on her own.

For a while, Louisa had wandered the Carlton House conservatory, eyeing the fan-vaulted ceiling above and the tropical flora below. Then, hoping for a cool breeze, she had strolled out to the garden, explored its florid pathways, and inhaled the scent of the roses. The prince's party of sycophants was keeping indoors today. The grounds were empty aside from a few workmen on the other end of the garden. From what Louisa could surmise, they were constructing stables to house Prince George's magnificent menagerie of horses, a collection funded by the prince's generous allowance from Parliament. She adored riding horses, herself. It was just one of the many accomplishments in which her tutors had trained her. But the horses, like little Princess Charlotte, were not in residence at present.

What can you possibly do with yourself until your father comes to fetch you?

She had seated herself on a stone bench that surveyed much of the garden. A tall wall shielded the royal garden from the public eye and the impudent public from the aristocratic one. This opulent garden with its stone pavilion and climbing trellises was not for the ordinary folk of London to enjoy. It was a private retreat for the upper class of the prince's circle.

Gurgle, gurgle, urgh! No matter how elegant and exotic Carlton House was, Louisa's complaining stomach reminded her that it did not make up for a missed meal and a missing parent.

Silly girl. You should have asked the prince's butler for some biscuits an hour ago. Why must you go on pretending that you don't need anything? That you don't need anyone?

Above the garden wall, Louisa could see the colonnade of trees that separated Carlton House's grounds from St. James' Park. Wafting above the stones came the faint clip-clop of carriage horses and the shouts of passers-by. St. James' Park was far less elegant than the gardens but far more lively at this time of day. A pity the wall was too high to watch the goings-on in the park—

No!

Louisa wrapped her arms around herself as tightly as a strait jacket at an asylum. There was no need to pine for a sight of the public park. How often must she remind herself that she enjoyed her own company best of all?

The sound of shoes scraping on stone caught her attention. Louisa scanned the horizon till she saw a mop of chestnut curls appear at the top of the wall. Someone was climbing into the Carlton House gardens!

Too surprised to be afraid, Louisa rose from the bench and strode toward the emerging intruder. At age sixteen, she was tall and well-proportioned and had almost reached the height of the average Englishman. She was mature enough to stand her ground against a stranger. "Who are you and what are you doing?"

The pleasant face of a young man only a few years older than her crested the wall. "I beg your pardon. I only wanted to see the garden." With an admirable display of strength, he pulled himself into a sitting posture on the top of the wall.

Louisa's violet-brown eyes narrowed. She assessed the young man's clean face, neat cravat, and proper waistcoat. He looked like an Oxford student getting up to a lark rather than a typical street ruffian searching for ill-gotten gains. But still, he was entering the prince's grounds uninvited....

"Now that you've seen it, you ought to go back the way you came. I'm certain that Prince George doesn't take kindly to trespassers."

"But I haven't seen the roses yet, and that's the reason I climbed up here."

Louisa's full lips set themselves into a firm line. "You'll be seeing the inside of Newgate if somebody catches sight of you." She filled her voice with authority. *She* was the daughter of the Duke of Warrenton and the Countess Dammartin. She would make him listen.

"*You've* caught sight of me, haven't you? I don't see you summoning the constables." Rotating his legs over the side of the wall, the young man began to lower himself into the royal grounds.

"Stop it this instant—" But Louisa's words came too late as his worn leather boots hit the grass with a soft thud.

"Just a peek at the rose garden, if you would be so kind, miss, and then I'll trouble you no further."

Shouldn't you summon the prince's footmen? That's what a sensible girl would do.

His brown eyes looked at her appealingly, and Louisa did not know whether to rebuke his presumption or admire his dogged persistence. He did not seem violent or unhinged—and he really was too handsome of a fellow to condemn to a fate like Newgate.

"Oh, very well," she said crossly, throwing up her hands as her French mother would have done. She would turn a blind eye to his lark. He inclined his head in silent gratitude and then hurried over to the rose garden.

Louisa followed him. Having allowed him entrance to the garden without outcry or public complaint, she almost felt as if it were her responsibility now to mind him like a beagle on a leash.

What if he is an anarchist? Or a French spy sent to assassinate the prince? Why are you letting yourself be taken in by a trim waistcoat and a neat cravat?

Once he reached the roses, the young man became so thoroughly engrossed that Louisa began to consider him more eccentric than dangerous. She watched him cradle one of the red blossoms in his fingers and noticed that he was measuring the length of the stalk against the span of his other hand. "One, two, three..."

Was he counting the petals now? What a peculiar individual! "What are you doing?"

He looked up with an abstracted smile. "This is a new variety to me. I want to discover how it is different from the Provence rose, so I am taking measurements and making some observations."

Louisa blinked. It was absurd, but his enthusiasm was beginning to make *her* wonder just what made that bush special. She had always assumed that a rose was a rose, but now he had given this flower another complexion entirely. "Why is it in a pot? I should think the gardener would want to plant it in the ground."

"I daresay he may want to move it into the conservatory in the wintertime, particularly if it is used to warmer climates. Sir Abraham Hume recommends the practice to all rosarians. If I had the means, I would plant all my rose bushes in pots."

Rosarians? So, there was a name *for this kind of eccentricity.*

"Do you possess a great many rose bushes?"

"Two dozen at our home in Derbyshire." He looked at her sheepishly. "My father has forbidden me from planting more."

As she had suspected, he was not yet of age and still under the tight rein of parental authority. She, on the other hand, had done exactly as she pleased ever since her mother had died eight years ago. "You're right. Two dozen is meagre indeed."

Her stomach gave an unladylike groan, reminding her how long she'd been enjoying the gardens without any tray of sandwiches to support her spirits. She watched as the young man moved on to the rose bush in the adjoining earthenware pot. "Do you mean to measure all these bushes?"

He nodded, not at all self-conscious. "Yes. You needn't watch if you find the activity dull."

"I do. Incredibly dull," said Louisa.

Liar! You know it was far, far duller here in the gardens before this handsome intruder arrived.

But Louisa's self-conceit was too great to admit any such thought aloud. "I shall leave you to it then."

Lifting her chin and turning on the heel of her trim half boots, Louisa strode down the path. She resisted the urge to see if the rosarian was watching her departure. Within a few moments, she arrived at the stone pavilion. Here was another place to sit. Here she could pretend that she was enjoying her trip to Carlton House and that the outing her father had planned for her was thoughtful and kind and tenderly paternal. Here she could effectively quash any interest in the chestnut-haired intruder.

Louisa had not rested long in the pavilion, however, before her solitude was invaded once again. This time, the intruder was someone who belonged at Carlton House—a member of the prince's set. His thinning red hair and pale white complexion looked strangely similar to Prince George's paramour inside the house, and his physique was not the kind that would lend itself to climbing over a garden wall. To Louisa, his thirty years seemed almost ancient. From his florid face, it was clear he had spent the afternoon indulging in something stronger than tea.

"Hallo there! And who might you be?" The man attempted to strike a pose by leaning against a pillar of the pavilion. But unfortunately, his balance bobbed precariously like a bottle in the ocean, and he almost fell on his posterior.

What a jackanapes!

Louisa rolled her eyes. Even at the young age of sixteen, she knew better than to introduce herself to a fellow that was foxed. She decided that mute hauteur was the better part of discretion.

"A silent Aphrodite, eh?" The man gave an effeminate titter mingled with a hiccough. "Egad! I never thought such a thing possible." Without warning, he stumbled over to the same bench on which she was sitting and sprawled beside her.

Disgusted, Louisa shifted away from him. But before she could abandon her place, the foppish fellow took hold of her arm and pulled her back down into her seat. Louisa stiffened like a larch tree and tried to control her rising panic. "Unhand me, you rude fellow." But even though he was drunk as a wheelbarrow, his grip was too strong to shake off.

"So, you do have a tongue?" The villain licked his lips. "But you've misplaced your manners. I'm an earl, doncha know?

Name's Yarmouth." His tittering mouth was far too close to her ear now. "I say, you're a pretty bird of paradise. White as a turtledove. I wager you'll coo for me." His hands were fumbling with the fabric of her dress now.

Silly girl. Why did you wear white? Let go, let go, let go!

Unable to free herself, Louisa felt the hunger in her stomach transform into a yawning chasm of fear. The encroaching earl attempted to pull her against his chest, and the fear transformed into fire. She was Lady Louisa Lymington, not some trollop like the painted ladies inside Carlton House. She willed her body to go limp as his disgusting lips began to nuzzle her cheek. Once he relaxed his hold, she would elbow him with all her force—

"Julia!" called a voice. "Julia! Oh, there you are!"

The young man from the rose garden entered the pavilion. Startled, the inebriated earl was shamefaced enough to let go of his quarry and slide over on the bench. "Good afternoon," said the young man earnestly. "I beg pardon for the sudden intrusion, but I've come to collect my little sister, Julia. Look here! I've gathered the rose clippings the prince promised us, but we must hurry. Cook has dinner ready at home, and our coach is waiting for us near the stables."

Dinner at home? Coach near the stables?

The young man with the mop of chestnut curls gave a careful nod to Louisa.

"Thank you, brother," said Louisa, trying to stop her knees from trembling. No doubt she would have been resourceful enough to extricate herself on her own, but the danger of the bygone moment did not escape her. She rose from the bench and crossed the pavilion hoping to take her rescuer's arm. His arms were full, however, and instead, he offered her some rose stems to carry. Without a backward glance at the gaping earl, they exited the stone pavilion and stepped into the sunlit gardens.

As soon as they were out of earshot of the pavilion, the young man gave her a concerned look. "Are you all right?"

All right? Why would he think you could possibly be "all right"?

"Perfectly," said Louisa, exercising her iron will to stop her legs from trembling. Her hands clutched like claws at the rose stems, and she could feel a thorn entering the soft skin of her index finger. Somehow, the pain was a blessing. It made her certain that this dream-like rescue was as real as gauze and sticking plaster. She pressed her thumb against the wound so that she would not drop blood on her white dress. She already felt stained. She would not add to it with literal blood.

"Do you have family here? Where shall I take you?"

"Nowhere," she said, ignoring the first of his questions. "I am perfectly able to take myself wherever I need to go."

"I beg your pardon," said the young man, with a half-smile. "I see my interruption was superfluous."

"No," said Louisa, grudgingly. "It was...welcome."

And unexpected. Unheard of. Unprecedented. You had better say nothing more about it, for he's likely regretting it already.

She looked down at the rose stems in her hands. "You're a bold one to steal plants from the prince's garden. What are these clippings for?"

His smile changed into an apologetic grin. "My garden in Derbyshire. I'll graft them onto other bushes in my garden." He explained away his theft with a bit of gardener's logic. "It doesn't hurt the plants, you know. They needed to be pruned anyway."

They had rounded the corner of the half-built stables now. None of the workmen challenged their presence, and they soon entered the carriage yard. The young man took the rose stems back from her, navigating the thorns skilfully as he layered them all in a bundle.

Louisa's finger throbbed miserably, and she wished it were ladylike to put it in her mouth and suck away the pain. A welcome sight in the carriage yard distracted her, however, as she spotted the Warrenton coachman. "Michael, harness up the horses, for I mean to go home now."

"Yes, my lady," said the surly fellow. "But what about his grace?"

That was his answer? What about his grace?

"You'll have to come back later for him."

Louisa could hear the coachman muttering under his breath as he brought the horses over to fasten them in their traces. She had no sympathy. The coachman was paid handsomely for his job of tooling the Warrenton carriage about London, and he had no call to complain about making two trips. "We will drop this young man off at his lodgings," instructed Louisa, adding yet another task to the coachman's list.

The young man took one look at the coat of arms painted on the carriage, and a look of doubt came into his eyes. "I'd best sit up in the carriage box."

Clearly, he is gentleman enough to know that he should not be in a closed carriage with you alone.

The difference between the young man's behaviour and the Earl of Yarmouth's boorishness was marked. The service this young man had rendered her was nothing short of heroic. And yet, he had done it as nonchalantly as if he regularly sauntered into royal gardens and saved white-gowned damsels every day after tea. And now he was trying to preserve her reputation even further.

"As you like," said Louisa with a shrug, trying to conceal her disappointment that their conversation would be curtailed. When Michael had finished harnessing the horses, Louisa listened as the young man gave the coachman the address for a hotel in the less fashionable part of town. Then, she allowed the young man to open the door for her as she climbed into the coach.

She cleared her throat. "I suppose I ought to ask your name."

That sounds far too eager. Do you really mean to appear so friendly?

She wanted very much to know who this fellow was to whom she was indebted, but her self-possession would not allow her to seem needy or dependent.

He shut the door carefully with one hand, maintaining hold of his rose clippings all the while. "Gyles."

That was it, then. No surname that would allow her to discover more about him. Just a simple "Gyles."

Will he ask your name in return? No, he seems far more interested in gathering up a rose stem fallen from his grasp.

"Good-bye, Gyles," said Louisa crisply, pulling back from the open window.

He looked up at her with a good-natured smile on his face, no doubt the same smile with which he greeted the butcher, the baker, or the vicar. "Good-bye, Julia." Then, with the same lithe grace that he had used in climbing the Carlton House wall, he swung himself up, one-handed, into the carriage box and the vehicle lurched into motion.

Thrown back into the corner of the seat, Louisa fumbled for her reticule and found a handkerchief inside. She pressed it against the wound on her finger. However beautiful the prince's garden might be, she knew from firsthand experience that all roses had their thorns. And one of the sharpest pricks she had endured that afternoon was that the gentleman who had saved her with his chivalry would not even take the time to ask after her name.

CHAPTER ONE

Incomparable

LONDON, ENGLAND ~ MAY 1810, FOUR YEARS LATER

"I SAY, AND I'VE always said, you're prime as punch, Lady Lou. D'ye think we ought to have a go of it together?"

Lady Lou? Prime as punch?

It was one of the less eloquent proposals that Louisa had received. She knew that Mr. Smythe, despite his happy-go-lucky charm, had been on tenterhooks all evening at the Mowbray ball, but even without a case of nerves, he was no Shakespeare. When it was their turn for a country dance, he had shuffled her over to an alcove instead, and there he laid his heart bare with this astonishingly inane proposal that they "have a go of it together."

"That's very kind of you, Mr. Smythe," said Louisa smoothly, more practised than Mr. Smythe at this sort of thing. After all, it was her fifth conquest in a highly successful debut season. As the Incomparable, she had become adept at responding to tongue-tied swains. "My uncle, as you know, is my guardian, so I think you'd best apply to him for permission."

"Oh, by Jove! I suppose I'd better." Mr. Smythe looked at her hopefully. "Then it's not a no, you mean?"

"I can't predict what my uncle will say, but if it were left up to me, I know where my affections lie."

That was vague enough to promise nothing and everything at the same time. You really are becoming a most excellent liar.

"Oh, by Jove!" said Mr. Smythe, again—lanky, loveable Mr. Smythe, whose head, unfortunately, contained far less wit than hair. His face lit up in sunny relief. "I'll call on him tomorrow. First thing!"

"See that you do," said Louisa with a cordial smile. It was a test. A trap. A corroboration of what she already suspected to be true. For although Mr. Smythe, who happened to live only a few houses away, would undoubtedly raise the knocker on the door of her Mayfair home, her uncle, the Duke of Warrenton, would undoubtedly send him away disappointed. He would dismiss Mr. Smythe's suit without consideration and then refrain from telling her that the man had even called.

It was not that her uncle was absent minded. No, he was as sharp as a card dealer from Soho and almost as untrustworthy. Over the course of the season, Louisa had been feted by admirers at every soiree, mobbed by suitors at every ball, and hailed as the Incomparable. And yet, according to her uncle, *no* offers of marriage had been made for her. It was incomprehensible. It was preposterous. It was too smoky by half.

She dismissed Mr. Smythe with a nod of her head and then looked out across the ballroom, trying to locate her uncle. There he was, leaning in rakishly to flirt with Lady Maltrousse. Louisa watched Uncle Nigel take the lady's fan and tease her by refusing to return it. She rolled her eyes. Of course, the lady was married—that seemed to be her uncle's preference. He was lucky he had not yet flirted with anyone who was *happily* married. Louisa would have enjoyed seeing her uncle's chiselled jaw crumple beneath a jealous husband's fist.

In her younger years, Louisa had always considered Uncle Nigel a good-hearted fellow. He had visited every year at Christmas and roasted apples and played at riddles with her. He had kept her company at dinner in the nursery while her parents dressed for dinners at other people's tables. But when he inherited the title, he had also inherited a desire to puff himself up in consequence. From the start, he had proceeded with the notion that the duties of a duke lay less in being a productive member of Parliament and more in being a fashionable rake about town. He had spent a preposterous amount of money and effort on playing a part, trying to prove himself just as much a dashing duke as Louisa's father had been.

Initially, he had been so involved with his own rackety affairs that he had hardly paid her any notice. When he had finally allowed her to make her come-out this season at the age of nineteen, he had barely interested himself in her. She had planned her presentation at court and her debut ball on her own and informed him what duties he would be required to perform. It was only after her success had been trumpeted throughout the *ton* that he had begun to take notice of her.

And you can see just where that notice has got you!

Tonight, he had offered to squire her to the Mowbray ball, and instead of disappearing into the card room, he was dividing his time between outrageous flirtation to create his own amusement and ghastly introductions to ruin Louisa's. In between dances, he had presented some of his more unsavoury connections to his niece. They were gentlemen twice her age with several strikes against them in appearance or behaviour. The Earl of Yarmouth, who had attempted to accost her four years ago, would have seemed a paragon compared to these undesirables. And unfortunately, this time, she had no mysterious rose gardener to fend off their attentions.

Louisa frowned as her uncle met her eye and returned Lady Maltrousse's fan. No doubt he meant to come her way again and introduce another "dear friend." Why on earth her uncle wanted to make her known to a pack of old *roués* was beyond her, but there was some sort of game afoot, and Louisa was determined to discover what it was.

She forced her brow to cease puckering and resumed the appearance of placid calm. She was fully aware that her serene, heart-shaped face was the foundation of her successful season and the adoration of her many suitors.

They think you're simple and sweet and serene. If they only knew what voices you have babbling inside your head. If they only knew what you thought of them all!

"Good evening, niece," said Uncle Nigel, grinning slyly and sliding his hand beneath her gloved elbow. "Are you enjoying yourself tonight?"

"I always do," said Louisa. And even more so when her uncle was absent! Uncle Nigel steered her towards the punch table. She would let him steer her for now, but she intended to take the rudder of her own fortunes into hand soon enough.

"It's quite a crush in here. Mowbray's circle of acquaintance is...extensive. Every baronet and his brother is here." Nigel spoke snidely as if his own taste in company were far more refined.

They reached the punch table, and he handed her a glass of the spiced liquid. Then, he cocked his head as if the idea had just come to him. "There's someone I want you to meet, Louisa. A new acquaintance of mine—Solomon Digby."

"Another acquaintance? I suppose he's one of the baronets littering the ballroom?"

"Er, no," said her uncle, glossing over the man's lack of title. "But he's quite congenial. And rich. You'll like him immensely."

"Will I indeed?" murmured Louisa. She had seen Mr. Digby announced at the door of the ballroom earlier in the evening. The grey-haired, pot-bellied fellow had repulsed her on sight. It was not so much his obesity that offended, but that he insisted on drawing attention to it with his garish puce and jonquil waistcoat.

"Let me make the introduction. And I should tell you in advance that I took the liberty of ceding him the supper dance that I wrote down on your dance card."

The pupils of Louisa's violet-brown eyes widened. "Did you indeed, uncle? Were you regretting spending dinner with me and planning to sit in Lady Maltrousse's pocket instead?"

"Of course not," said her uncle, without even the decency to blush. "I was merely looking out for your own amusement. Mr. Digby will keep you entertained."

Louisa almost snorted aloud in disbelief. She was certain that the only entertainment Mr. Digby would provide at dinner was coarse talk and rude stares. She would have to do her best to quell any familiarity.

By now, she was used to the fact that if she did not look out for herself, no one would. Parents lived and died. Servants came and went. Only *she* was a constant in her own life. Only *she* could be trusted to keep herself safe. She had her uncle's measure now, and she was determined to find out why he was so intent on foisting his fusty friends on her instead of securing a suitor like Mr. Smythe, and why her season as the Incomparable has been so incomparably dissatisfying.

Chapter Two

Licence

Mr. Smythe did *not* call on the house—or, at least, that was Louisa's uncle's story when she asked him a few days later. The truth of the matter, which was easily obtainable after passing a shilling to a footman, was that Mr. Smythe *had* called and had been sent packing while she was engaged in a painting lesson with her art tutor. Just like her other non-existent suitors, he had been summarily dismissed before she could receive word of it.

What game is Uncle Nigel playing? Does he mean to keep you on the shelf forever?

Some parents might reject their daughter's suitors because of a sentimental attachment and a wish to keep their darling daughter a little longer. But Louisa did not flatter herself that her uncle *enjoyed* her company. Their opinions clashed on everything, from which paper-hangings to place on the drawing room wall to which menus to order from Cook. No, if she could be got rid of, Uncle Nigel would be delirious with joy to have the townhouse to himself. So why did he persist in turning away all eligible suitors?

The matter became clear to her the following week when she overheard fat-bellied Solomon Digby scheming with her uncle in the billiards room. She had gone to the library to fetch a book—something tedious enough to lull her to sleep after a dull night at Almack's—and she overheard voices in the room next to the library. Stepping lightly in her kid slippers, Louisa approached the library door and put an ear to the cold keyhole.

"A hundred thousand pounds, you say?"

"Exactly," said her uncle with a sigh, "and I can't touch a penny of it myself. It's really most unfair. All I received from my brother was an estate encumbered with *his* debts. And my niece has the whole fortune from her mother sewn up in a silk purse."

Louisa knew that her father had left the Warrenton estate in disgraceful disarray, but that knowledge was not enough to make her sympathise with her uncle. He must accept the hand of cards that he had been dealt. They all must.

Odious Mr. Digby let out an oath. "Stap me, yer grace! When she comes of age, she'll be the richest gel in London."

"Yes," said her uncle meaningfully. "Or her husband will be."

Husband?

At that word, Louisa felt a thunderbolt of fury go straight to her breast. She had sharp enough wits to know which direction the conversation was tending. She pressed her ear to the door of the billiards room more tightly and heard her uncle propose to promote Digby's interest with her if the fellow would split the dowry with him.

"A pity she's my niece," said Uncle Nigel, "or I'd marry her myself and take the whole hundred thousand pounds. But as the matter stands, what do you say to half the inheritance?"

Are they really planning to carve up your mother's bequest up like a Cornish game hen?

Louisa's fingers clenched into fists. Her mother had died when Louisa was eight years old, leaving her with an inheritance of fluent French, a cache of expensive jewellery, and an account full of English banknotes. Although she had never consulted directly with a solicitor, Louisa was aware that on her twenty-first birthday, she would be wealthy indeed.

"Fifty thousand pounds *and* a prime filly?" said Digby, his wet lips smacking together audibly. "I'll take it. Gladly."

Louisa heard brandy being decanted and glasses clinking as they sealed their nefarious bargain. Careful not to make a sound, she backed away from the door of the billiards room. It was well she knew of her uncle's plan, for it would give her more occasion to thwart him. He would find out soon enough that the daughter of the Countess Dammartin was more than a match for the new Duke of Warrenton.

⁓

Mr. Digby became a regular dinner guest at their Mayfair home. Over the soup and souffles, Louisa attempted to ignore his crude insinuations with icy hauteur. Over the veal and venison, she tried to quell his ingratiating manner with scornful disdain. But Mr. Digby had no pride to be wounded when fifty thousand pounds were on the line. No hint enlightened him. No snub deterred him. He simply grinned a self-satisfied smile that covered both his chins and tried again to pat her hand.

Social events outside of their town house were no better. Every time Louisa turned around, the disgusting Mr. Digby was at her elbow. She was beginning to lose all pleasure in rout parties and ridottos, for as soon as she left her house she was dogged by a persistent and ponderous presence that threatened her self-possession and shattered her serenity.

The following week, her uncle was in particularly good spirits. He had bought a new curricle and a new pair of horses and seemed to be flashing about an enormous amount of cash. Louisa was no bookkeeper, but she had a good head on her shoulders. For Uncle Nigel to have a large sum on his hands was peculiar, to say the least. She knew that the Warrenton estate was all rolled up after her father had finished with it and dry as a bone after her uncle had sucked out the remaining marrow. "Where did you get the money, uncle? Gambling?"

"Of a sort," he said with a laugh. "Digby's loaned it to me, an advance on a payment I'll be making to him."

Having heard the conversation in the billiards room, Louisa was well aware what that payment would be. She decided to speak plainly with her uncle, or at least as plainly as prudence dictated. "I don't like Solomon Digby. I wish you'd stop associating with him. He's not good ton. You'd never see Viscount Landsdowne or the Earl of Kendall shaking hands with such a lout."

Uncle Nigel stiffened. "Landsdowne and Kendall received both a title *and* a silver spoon. They can afford to be more squeamish than I can. I'll associate with whomever I need to, Louisa, and you'll put a pretty face on matters and be polite."

"I can't be polite to a man I detest."

"Oh, I know you're a superb actress when you want to be. So, act! Act like you like him, Louisa, for I've borrowed two thousand pounds from him, and it will not go well with me if I don't repay it."

Louisa's aristocratic eyes flashed. "The more fool you, uncle."

Her uncle moved toward her menacingly. "Would you be more compliant if your amusements were taken away? No more theatre? No more Almack's? No more Vauxhall? Hmm?"

"Do what you like," said Louisa. She had turned twenty halfway through this season, and she would come of age partway through the next. She could wait out her uncle's displeasure for a year until he lost the role of guardian. Then, no matter how he complained, she could decamp from the Warrenton townhouse to her own establishment. She could find some ancient aunt or distant cousin to be her obligatory chaperone instead of Uncle Nigel. She could finally visit Paris if she pleased and see the place her mother had called home. She could set the tone of the ton and aristocratic society as she had always known she would. A year was long, but not too long when she had the rest of her life to live.

Her uncle was as good as his threat. Since Louisa refused to countenance the suitor of his choice, he gave it out that she was indisposed and cancelled all her engagements. The only caller admitted to the house was Solomon Digby. Day in and day out, Louisa never knew when she might be surprised by those heavy jowls and wide waistcoat. And no matter how much she glowered or snapped at him, she could still feel his lecherous gaze settle on her approvingly.

Mr. Digby stayed late after dinner one night, and after pretending to retire for the evening, Louisa slipped down to the billiards room keyhole once again.

"You don't seem to have captured her fancy yet," she heard her uncle remark morosely.

"What do you mean?" Mr. Digby said in surprise. "The chit's intrigued by me, I can tell. She simply likes to play games to pretend she has the upper hand."

"So...you think she'd accept you if you were to put the question to her?"

Perhaps her uncle was beginning to have his doubts about winning her over. Perhaps he was starting to wonder just how he was going to repay Solomon Digby when Louisa refused to come up to scratch.

"Who knows?" said Mr. Digby. "She might think it amusing to continue to be coy. But a special licence would salvage the situation, eh?"

"Yes, I suppose it would, but would the archbishop really ever grant such a—"

"Write me an affy-davy of her eligibility, and I'll get one," said Digby confidently. He had boasted at dinner of the mint of money he had made in trade and of the unscrupulous dealings he had used to beat out competitors. No doubt he had the money needed for a special licence and knew just which strings of influence to pull. "And I'll also find a vicar who's not too nice about matters and willing to do the ceremony out of the public eye for an extra fee."

Louisa backed away from the door with a growing sense of indignation. A special licence would mean that they could spring the marriage upon her in her own drawing room. Even if she screamed her refusal, her uncle would find some way to muzzle her and make her go through with the ceremony. Tiptoeing down the corridor, she made her way upstairs. Hopefully, it would take some time for Mr. Digby to obtain a special licence and a venal vicar, for she needed some time as well to plan a successful escape.

CHAPTER THREE

Gardener

DERBYSHIRE, ENGLAND ~ MAY 1810

GYLES AUDELEY SWUNG A mattock to break up the dirt clods in his new garden bed. The coarse red soil had a good deal of clay in it, and it often took a whole afternoon to plant just three rose bushes. The three he was planting today were replicas of others in the garden—raised from cuttings he had taken last year. He took peculiar pride in having the largest rose garden roundabouts, with over three hundred rose bushes, and he aspired to expand his domain into the largest rose garden in Derbyshire.

He lifted the spade and began to dig the deep hole necessary to house the root ball for the first rose bush. The new bushes would not bloom this summer, of course. It took some time after transplant for a bush to really thrive. But he had high hopes that this was the year for his Sweet-Scented China Rose to bloom. The esteemed botanist Sir Abraham Hume had sent him cuttings for it a year and a half ago, and it was well past time to see the fruit of his labours with that bush.

"Oi there, Mr. Audeley," said a pert voice. Gyles looked up. "Might ye be needin' some help with that diggin'?"

"Hello, Archie," said Gyles, wiping a bead of sweat from his brow. Archie Garrick, the nephew of their butler, was tall as a beanstalk, spotted as a toadstool, and as ubiquitous as flies in a cow pasture. A few years younger than Gyles, the fellow had set his heart on entering service at the Audeleys' manor house. But Gyles and his mother had no need for a footman, and they already possessed a coachman and a butler. "No, thank you, I have the digging well in hand."

"Looks like ye have a spade in hand, Mr. Audeley. I could help wi' that, and ye could twiddle yer thumbs and admire yer garden."

Gyles grimaced. Twiddling his thumbs was the last thing he wanted to do in pleasant weather. The smell of the freshly turned earth and the warmth of the air invigorated him like a heady elixir. It was his privilege and pleasure to serve as gardener for his country estate, and he had no intention of turning over his job to Archie Garrick.

"That will be unnecessary." Gyles' foot stamped the spade into the ground again.

"Well then," said Archie, realising his overtures were unlikely to be received that day, "another time, Mr. Audeley. I could fix yer rose garden up right pretty-like. I've been watchin' you trim them, and I know just how's you like them."

Gyles strongly doubted that Archie had any clear concept of how to prune a rose bush, but being a peaceable man, he nodded without argument.

As the sun rose higher in the sky, Mrs. Audeley brought out a pitcher of cool liquid with a glass for her son. He put the spade down and gratefully took a gulp of lemonade. Then, giving the glass back to her, he knelt in the dirt to pull some stones out of the hole he had dug.

His mother lingered, watching him, until she could contain herself no longer. "Gyles! I've thought of the best plan. Should you like to take a house in London at the end of the summer? You would get to see the flowers at Kew Gardens and meet ever so many famous botanists. And I could perchance do some shopping?"

The sun was right behind her, and Gyles squinted upwards while rubbing dirty hands on his old buckskins. London? Shopping? What was this harebrained scheme she had hatched? They'd not been to London for four years...not since Father had died. Following his father's demise, his widowed mother had continued as she had always done, keeping a neat house and a full table and a quiet presence here in the country. He had always supposed she was as content as he was to remain in Derbyshire.

"I daresay *you* might take a house in London whenever you like, Mother. But I shall stay here in Derbyshire. Otherwise, who would take care of the roses?" The last time he had left his home, he'd only abandoned two dozen rose bushes, but now that Audeley House belonged to him, his garden held even more bushes than the prince's gardens at Carlton House.

"Surely you can find someone to water them," said his mother, with the naive innocence borne of someone who did not garden herself. As if watering were the only thing that must be done! If that were the case, then spotty-faced Archie Garrick would be a proper caretaker. "And besides, you would get to meet Sir Abraham Hume in person."

Gyles rubbed his nose with the cleanest of his knuckles. He was perfectly content with his current level of acquaintance with the botanist. Gyles had first written Sir Abraham two years ago when he had reached the age of majority. They now conducted a regular correspondence by post, but it was immaterial to him whether he ever met the man face to face. He supposed such indifference might stem from growing up as an only child. He was used to his own company, and he never felt the need for companionship that afflicted others so strongly.

"I'm sorry to disappoint you, Mother, but I can't leave Derbyshire during the summer months." He refrained from promising her a London visit during the winter months instead. There was still so much to do with wintering the rose bushes and preparing the ground for spring. He hated the idea of abandoning his garden no matter the season. The last time he had gone to London at the age of nineteen he had obtained some new varieties to cultivate, but his small garden had been in such disarray when he returned, that he disliked the idea of leaving it ever again. And besides, he was currently working on the larger project of writing down all his endeavours with ink on paper. Someday, other rose gardeners would benefit from his record of plantings, prunings, failures, and successes.

"I have high hopes that my Sweet-Scented China Rose will bloom this summer. I'm sorry, Mother, but it just isn't possible for me to go to London."

"I understand." His mother's fleeting look of disappointment lasted an instant, but then she moved on to another idea. "Perhaps we might simply hold a dinner party next month?"

Gyles got to his feet. "Whom would we invite?" This part of Derbyshire was not particularly well populated with families of the gentry. The late Mr. Audeley had been content to lead a staid and boring existence on his land outside of Upper Cross, and they had rarely entertained guests.

"Oh," said Mrs. Audeley, distractedly, "I thought we might have Mr. and Mrs. Brownlee, and the vicar and his wife. And then perhaps Miss Morrison? You like her, don't you?"

Gyles raised an eyebrow. Miss Morrison was a gentlewoman farmer a mile or more down the lane. No doubt his mother supposed that Miss Morrison, with her interest in agriculture, would be a good match for him, but their nearby neighbour was more interested in crop rotation and seed drills than she was in beauty. And although Gyles might deplore society and the metropolis, beauty was as necessary to him as air.

"Miss Morrison is very unexceptionable," said Gyles. "I appreciate her as much as you do, I suppose." It was tepid praise, calculated to give his mother pause.

"Hmm, yes." Mrs. Audeley's eyes melted into a look of resignation. "Well, a dinner party does seem like a good deal of trouble. I shall think of something else."

"Whatever you think best, Mother." Thankful that she was giving up her plans as soon as she had proposed them, Gyles turned his attention back to the soil. He wanted his mother to be happy. He certainly would let her go to town if she were fixed on the idea. He would order her new dresses and bonnets. He would even entertain Miss Morrison at dinner if it gave his mother pleasure. But to leave his garden was a sacrifice of a higher order.

This hole was almost big enough for the root ball of his largest transplant. He would move a few more rocks and then set the plant in place. But as for transplanting himself for a season, he had no intention of doing anything of the kind. He was perfectly content to be a country gentleman with no adventures beyond those afforded by heat, drought, rain, and sunshine.

CHAPTER FOUR

Preparation

LONDON, ENGLAND ~ JUNE 1810

*P*ARIS—THE CITY OF LOVE. *You might find someone there who understands you, for you certainly haven't found him in London. Or at least someone who will marry you and let you be and let you cultivate your own circle of admirers. That's the kind of marriage your parents had, and they were happy enough.*

Louisa had always wanted to visit the place of her mother's birth, but even though some travel still took place between the warring nations, her distracted father had possessed no interest in braving Boney's dragoons. "'Pon rep, Lou-Lou! That Bonaparte's as full of hot air as one of those balloon contraptions. There's no telling whether these Frenchies might confuse the Duke of Warrenton with the Duke of Wellington. And then where would I be, I ask you?"

The possibility of her foppish father being confused with the hero of England had always seemed a remote eventuality, but Louisa had been forced to give up the idea of Paris for the time being. She had learned long ago that the world was a swing that went up and down with her father's mood.

But now that her father was no longer there to object, Louisa considered the matter again. Should she flee to Paris to escape Mr. Digby's nefarious designs? Napoleon's role as emperor there was no deterrent to *her*, but the difficulty of making a Channel crossing during wartime gave her pause. She wondered how prudent it would be for one who looked so much an Englishwoman to venture to France without male escort. With her golden hair and skin of cream and roses, she would stand out amidst the dark-haired belles of Paris ballrooms. She wondered how unusual it would be for an unmarried woman to set up her own establishment on one of Paris' many boulevards. She wondered how difficult it would be to undertake a Channel passage and then a journey from the French coast to the French metropolis.

After much thought, Louisa discarded the idea of fleeing to France as too impulsive and too impossible without an accomplice. But what other options were available to her? A quick perusal of *The Times* revealed several advertisements for governess positions. There was one in particular which caught her eye: a situation with three female charges in the northern county of Yorkshire.

Louisa cut out the advertisement with a pair of scissors and burned the rest of the page. If she disappeared suddenly, there was no point in leaving a trail of evidence for Uncle Nigel to find. After composing a careful reply in the secrecy of her bedchamber, she carried her letter to the post herself. *That* was a new experience for her, but it would have been the height of absurdity to ask her uncle to frank the letter or to leave it on the tray for a footman. She wanted no questions about why she was writing to Yorkshire.

Now she had only to wait for the return post and pray for success. Yorkshire would be far enough removed that her uncle would never find her, and with any luck, she could live out the rest of her minority there until she could claim her inheritance in her own right.

No more Uncle Nigel to worry about. No more Mr. Digby. You'll be free at last to take care of yourself.

While she waited for an answer to her letter, however, Mr. Digby was continuing to pose a problem. His hints about Louisa's desirability had become so monstrously alarming that she was certain the trap would be sprung this very week. If Mr. Digby had the special licence in hand, then it only meant that her own plan must be put into action sooner. She could not wait for an acceptance. She must simply assume that the governess position was hers and travel to Yorkshire to take it.

To fob off any suspicion of her flight, Louisa forced herself to be civil to both Mr. Digby and her uncle at dinner on Thursday.

"Such a charming waistcoat you are wearing tonight, Mr. Digby." The lie sounded false, even to her own ears as she gazed at the aquamarine monstrosity over the first remove.

Mr. Digby gave a ponderous sigh of satisfaction. *Ugh!* If she ever heard such a thing again, she would cut off her own ears.

"You are too kind, milady. Too kind." His jowls shook as he spoke, and Louisa felt specks of spittle travelling across the dining table.

"Louisa's *always* the kindest of women," said her uncle approvingly. It was yet another clue that something suspicious was afoot, for when in the last two years had Uncle Nigel ever been so complimentary?

"Will you play the pianoforte for us after dinner?" asked Mr. Digby, taking a drink and swishing his wine about in his mouth before he swallowed. "I'm not much for music myself, but I can turn the pages."

The idea of Mr. Digby brushing her shoulder as he fumbled for the music was as nauseating as spoiled asparagus. "I'm afraid I have a bit of a headache," apologised Louisa. "Unfortunately, I will have to retire early."

It took much convincing and additional protestations of ill health on her part, but eventually Uncle Nigel let her bid an early goodnight. Once safely in her room, she commenced her plan in earnest. She had already taken the precaution of obtaining all her jewellery from the safe and had sewn the necklaces and bracelets into the hem of her cloak and the lining of her bonnet. She had a good eye for jewels and could tell that these pieces from her mother were worth a great deal of money. At least it had not come into Uncle Nigel's head yet to try pawning them. The chief difficulty would come in getting her trunk from her bedroom on the first floor to the outside street where she could hail a hackney. Louisa was tall and well-formed, but she did not have the strength a man would use to heft the trunk. It was a large one and stuffed full like a sausage casing. She had packed it with all her most serviceable dresses—as well as a few more elaborate creations. A woman's clothing was her armour, and she would need all the protection she could muster in the wilds of Yorkshire.

Since she could not carry the trunk herself, it would be necessary to let a footman in on her secret.

But which one? Can you really trust any of them?

She had never cultivated any familiarity with the domestics. Even the ones who had been there for years were more attached to their quarterly wages than they were to the lady of the house.

As she trailed her fingers along the bannister, Louisa considered the footmen standing in the entrance hall below. Three of them, unaware of observation, were speaking jokingly with each other while one stood off from the rest, aloof, unincluded. He was an outsider. Just like she was. That would be the fellow to choose.

Later that night, after her fictitious headache had subsided, Louisa announced that her sitting room furniture needed re-arrangement. She sent her confused lady's maid to fetch the aloof footman, and once she had him alone, negotiated a rate for the surreptitious service of hauling her trunk down the back staircase in the early morning hours.

"Your uncle will cut up rough when he finds out," replied the footman. He pocketed the earnest money of one shilling that she offered him.

"Perhaps he will," said Louisa, her perfect pink lips set into a firm line, "but I'm sure you're too clever to admit that you were involved with my departure."

"Course I am," said the footman smugly, puffing out his chest. She fixed a steely look on him. "My lady," he concluded in grudging respect, tugging his forelock before he left the room.

❧

Midnight and the conspiratorial footman were a long time coming. The moon had been up for hours before Louisa heard him scratching like a rat on the outside of her door. Swiftly, she opened it, her tall figure cloaked in warm woollen navy, a solitary candle in her hand to light the enterprise. She nodded toward the trunk at her feet. The footman lifted it onto his shoulder with a barely suppressed grunt. Then it was down the stairs with hushed footsteps, Louisa lighting the way, until they reached the lower floor.

Louisa had no intention of risking egress through the front door. Instead, she led the footman to the back of the house, put down her candle, and used her ring of keys to open a small door that led out into the stable yard. "Down the alley and around the corner," she whispered.

"All that way? What d'ye have in this trunk, my lady?" he grumbled quietly. "Rocks?"

Louisa ignored his complaints. She had promised him five pounds, an excessively generous reward for toting a trunk three hundred yards. With the footman trailing behind her, she made her way through the stable yard and out to the side street. There, she hailed a hackney.

This hackney, however, had a fare already inside. As Louisa shrunk back into the shadows, she saw long, lanky Mr. Smythe descend onto the pavement. When he saw her, he stumbled abruptly. Apparently, he was in his cups—a state in which Louisa never hoped to observe Mr. *Digby*.

"I say there," he said, his midnight vision surprisingly acute for one in his condition. "S'that Lady Lou?" He veered closer to her as if his will was not entirely in control of his legs. "What're you doing outside this time a'night?" He hiccoughed loudly.

"Oh, please, Mr. Smythe," Louisa whispered fiercely. "You must keep quiet." She looked at his simple, inebriated face and took a calculated risk. "I'm running away from home, and you mustn't tell my uncle."

"Runnin' away?" Mr. Smythe was almost shocked into so-briety by that statement, but the fuzziness of a half-bottle of brandy soon overcame him once again. "That's a bit of a shurprise. He said you weren't keen on me. But didn't know you were that set against it. Runnin' away and all."

"No, no, Mr. Smythe," said Louisa, raising an arm and waving so that the hackney driver would not lose interest in her and drive away. "I am certainly not running away because of *you*. There's someone else—someone much worse. And I'm determined not to accept him, and so, you see, I must leave."

"Ah, another blighter," said Mr. Smythe, nodding sagely as if he understood. "Worsh than me. Makes perfect shense. An' i' thish your trunk?" He blinked at the footman, the street lamp gleaming off the whites of his eyes.

"Yes, that's it," said Louisa hurriedly. She beckoned to the footman to tie the trunk on the back of the hackney.

"You musht allow me to ashist," said Mr. Smythe. With surprising agility, he took the trunk from the footman and tied it to the back of the public carriage. Louisa gave the grumbling footman his five pounds, and he retreated down the alley to the Lymington townhouse. Hopefully, he would keep his word and keep quiet to her uncle about her depar-ture.

Louisa negotiated her fare and destination with the driver. Impelled by his chivalrously intoxicated instincts, Mr. Smythe came round the hackney to open the door for her. As he did so, however, an alarm bell of warning began to sound in his muddled head. "Now see here, Lady Lou. It's not shafe for a lady to dishappear in th' dead of night. Where're you going to, anyway?"

"That is none of your affair. Good-bye, Mr. Smythe."

As her erstwhile suitor gaped and waved, Louisa climbed into the hackney and closed the door. The driver would take her to the nearest posting house, and with any luck, she would secure a seat in the morning post up the Great North Road to the Earl of Kendall's estate in Yorkshire.

CHAPTER FIVE

Barrowby Park

YORKSHIRE, ENGLAND ~ JUNE 1810

THREE DAYS LATER, AFTER a journey of marvellously cramped quarters, hitherto unknown smells, and far too loquacious fellow passengers, Louisa arrived at her destination. There was no one waiting for her at the Yorkshire posting inn. It could not be otherwise, for no one at Lord Kendall's house was expecting her arrival.

Undeterred, Louisa took out a few shillings and asked the innkeeper to find her a man with a cart who could bring her and her trunk to Barrowby Park. She had made it this far without being duped, robbed, or ravished by any rogues of the road. She had no intention of waiting on chance now. One must make one's own luck in the world, and Louisa was used to seizing the day.

A farmer with a dogcart offered to take the pretty miss up to the big house, free of charge, and Louisa soon found herself at the steps of a large Palladian manor house with her brass-bound trunk on the ground beside her. She took a deep breath. What now? A governess was not a servant. She had every right to knock on the front door.

"May I help you, miss?" A grey-haired butler stared down at her. His manner was not unkind, but the door was hardly opened in an inviting manner. Louisa reflected on the difference of reception a lady received when arriving in a farmer's dogcart rather than in a carriage with a ducal escutcheon.

"I'm Miss Lymington, here to respond to the governess advertisement."

"Ah," said the butler, opening the door a little wider. "I was not aware that his lordship had begun interviews yet for that position. But yes, yes, come in, and I will let Lord Kendall know that you are here."

Relieved to have made it past the first gatekeeper, Louisa entered the house and took a seat in the hall. It was strange not to be ushered straight into the drawing room, but it was something to which she would have to accustom herself. She had never paid much heed to the position of her own governesses, but thinking back on the matter, she recalled that they had never received the same privileges as members of the family.

She wondered if Lord Kendall would recognise her. He had been conspicuously absent from ton events this season as she made her debut, but she had followed the aristocratic circles for years, and she knew him by sight and by reputation. Her father had always spoken of him as an infuriatingly put-together fellow, blessed with title, looks, address, and funds. The latter quality was one which had always eluded the Lymington men.

The name *Kendall* was not a favourite in the Warrenton house. Mentioning Lord Kendall was a sure way to set Uncle Nigel's back up, and Louisa had oftentimes gained a revenge on her uncle by expatiating on how poorly he compared to the dapper earl from Yorkshire. Louisa guessed that Lord Kendall was much of an age with her uncle, but from the pleasant tone of the advertisement, he was taking a far friendlier interest in his orphaned nieces than *her* uncle had taken in her.

"Miss Lymington," said Lord Kendall, standing to acknowledge her presence as the butler announced her at the door of the study. It was a good sign, indicating that a governess would be treated respectfully in this household. "The name seems familiar. Have we met before?"

Louisa's velvety eyes assessed him frankly. His black hair was just beginning to show streaks of silver, and although he was twice her age, his figure was firm and strong and had not run to fat. "I don't believe so, my lord." She remembered her position half a second later and bobbed a curtsy.

Lord Kendall gestured to a chair and then seated himself again behind his desk. Louisa sat down and straightened her serviceable brown skirt.

"I had not yet responded to your letter, Miss Lymington, so it is strange that you would travel here for an interview without an invitation."

"Oh, there must have been some mistake, my lord. I *had* a letter from you, I'm certain of it. Perhaps your secretary sent it without your knowledge?"

What a taradiddle! Do you really think he will believe that?

"Hmm. Richards is forgetful, but not *that* forgetful. May I see the letter?"

Louisa opened her reticule to search for the fictitious letter but, naturally, emerged from the search empty-handed. "It must have fallen out in the mail coach."

"Hmm," said Lord Kendall again as if he did not trust the veracity of that statement. "Well, here you are, in any case." His bright blue eyes looked at her searchingly. "You are very young. How old are you?"

"Five and twenty," Louisa lied glibly.

"Indeed?" His eyebrows arched in surprise. "Have you worked as a governess previously?"

"Yes, here are my references." Louisa had taken the precaution of drawing up two fictitious letters from society ladies who had children of suitable ages. She hoped Lord Kendall was not familiar enough with their households to question the veracity of the letters.

She held her breath until his eyes had finished skimming the papers, but he asked no clarifying questions about her past charges.

"This letter says that you speak Italian. Is that correct?"

"And French," said Louisa. "Fluently." The descriptions of her qualifications, even though written by herself, were true without a hint of embellishment. Her father had procured a constant string of governesses and instructors for her throughout her adolescence, and as she could never stand to do anything poorly, she had excelled at languages, painting, music, dancing, and everything else a young lady was expected to master.

Lord Kendall regarded her thoughtfully. "My nieces are woefully deficient in all subjects. There is still time for Milly, I suppose, since she's only nine years old, but Ginny has only one more year in the schoolroom and Penny is due to come out this year in London."

"A daily course of study can achieve much in the matter of months," said Louisa encouragingly. She had no idea how apt these girls were, but she was determined that Lord Kendall would not turn her away from this Yorkshire sanctuary. She *must* hide herself away here until she came of age. "I am particularly good at motivating young ladies to succeed."

Lord Kendall gave a wry grin. "Ah, well, I think you'll find it difficult to motivate Penny to do anything if she takes a dislike to you. Ginny and Milly are more reasonable." He tapped his fingers against the desk and considered her. "Are you sure we have not met before, Miss Lymington?"

"I don't think so, my lord," said Louisa demurely.

Surely, he will not spoil everything by recognizing you now?

He cleared his throat. "Very well, I suppose you might attempt the position. It will save me the trouble of interviewing other governesses, and perhaps Penny will learn better from someone closer to her age. Or if it's too late for Penny, at least you can do something with Milly and Ginny. If you're willing, I'll request the housekeeper prepare a room for you, and you'll begin in the morning."

Louisa inclined her head regally, recalling her subservient position a fraction of a second later and following that up with a meek, "Yes, my lord."

Chapter Six

Needed

Derbyshire, England ~ July 1810

"Oh, hallo there!" called a pleasant voice from the edge of the lane as twilight was coming on. "Have you seen my magpie cat?"

Gyles lowered his pruning shears. "Hello, Miss Morrison. No cats here, I'm afraid." Inwardly, he gave a silent prayer of gratitude. He had no desire for cat excrement in his flower beds, and he was happy that he'd seen no black and white felines slinking through his rose garden. If he had, he would have hired Archie Garrick on the spot to drive the creatures away.

"Oh dear," said Miss Morrison. "She always goes so far afield when she is breeding. I never know where she'll end up with the kittens when they come." Miss Morrison was much like her cat, Gyles reflected, for she was quite far afield without a bonnet or gloves. But then again, her wiry brown hair was never covered with a bonnet, and her arms were as tanned as his were by the sunshine and exposure to the elements.

"You could keep her indoors," suggested Gyles. He opened the shears and clipped off a wilted white rose so that others could grow back in its place.

Miss Morrison wrinkled her nose. "She wouldn't much care for that. And neither would I!" She looked up at the sky where the blue was beginning to purple. "The weather's been fine lately, and I'm looking forward to the early harvest next month. Did you finally put in some spring barley this year, Mr. Audeley?"

"Er...no," said Gyles. "I'm busy with other things."

"Roses, you mean?"

"Exactly."

Miss Morrison was always inquiring about his crops. She seemed to think that cultivating roses was a waste of an opportunity better used for beans or oats or wheat. "Some of your tenants put in a good crop of barley."

"Yes, that's their prerogative."

"But if *you* used your land to the best of its ability then your estate would be a good deal more profitable—"

"My mother and I live simply, Miss Morrison. We are in no need of additional income."

She looked at him dubiously. Gyles took a deep breath and clipped another rose. After receiving one of Miss Morrison's lectures, he always felt that he had disappointed her. She was a friendly enough woman, but he could not keep pace with her frenetic energy. The blasted woman walked her fields daily and gave direct commands to her own labourers, rather than using a steward as an intermediary. She kept the books for her own crops and went to market with her own wheat. She had the yield of her acreage memorised down to a quarter bushel.

Gyles knew that his mother would love for him to further his acquaintance with Miss Morrison, but the idea of attaching himself to such a self-sufficient and utilitarian creature was unappealing. No, if Gyles Audeley ever lost his heart to a female, it would be to one who needed him like a rose garden needs the rain. He could put up with a few thorns and prickles for the sake of beauty...not barley.

"I'll wish you good evening," said Miss Morrison brightly, "and if you do see my cat, send a servant round, please. She's a good mouser, and I would hate to lose her."

There was the reason for the cat at last. The cat was a good mouser, and that was why she'd come in search of it. Miss Morrison was certainly not one to keep a pet for the purpose of pampering it or for the sake of affection. "Of course. Good evening, Miss Morrison."

"And let me know if your mother wants one of the kittens!" she called out as an afterthought.

Gyles waved his shears noncommittally and went back to his pruning. If he had interpreted his mother's oblique hints correctly, his mother wanted grandchildren, not kittens. And he was unlikely to provide either of them anytime soon.

CHAPTER SEVEN

Governess

YORKSHIRE, ENGLAND ~ JULY 1810

LOUISA FLIPPED THROUGH THE book of French grammar and began to read aloud. The second chapter was on introductions, something any well-bred lady would often encounter, particularly if she ever travelled to Paris. It was supremely useful and supremely elegant.

"To introduce yourself by name, the pronoun *je* should be employed along with a reflexive verb—"

The eldest Miss Trafford folded her arms and sighed.

"If you would be so good as to listen in silence," said Louisa.

"I don't know why we should be expected to learn such a silly language," replied Penelope Trafford with a huff. "Half the letters aren't even pronounced, and the ones that *are* seem to be stuck in your nose like a bad cold."

"French is the language of cosmopolitan society," said Louisa in rebuke. Her fingers clenched involuntarily around the grammar book. The last four weeks had been some of the most trying days of her life. She had always tolerated her tutors, mostly because she had nothing else to do with her day but to listen to them. But the eldest Miss Trafford had done everything in her power to thwart and upend Louisa's inaugural lessons. The girl wasted no opportunity to disrupt a drawing session, argue about a point of etiquette, or sabotage a pianoforte practice.

The younger two girls, considered by themselves, were not unbearable. In time, Louisa thought she might come to enjoy Milly's precociousness and Ginny's slow-moving sweetness. But Penny, who was only a year and a half younger than Louisa, had flaunted her displeasure from the first. Even during the lessons where Lord Kendall had been present, Penny had bridled and bucked like an unbroken pony.

Louisa was insightful enough to discern that Penny's dislike for her stemmed directly from the girl's dislike for her own guardian. Since Lord Kendall had hired Miss Lymington, Miss Trafford was determined to detest the governess. And since Lord Kendall was a "heartless and unfeeling tyrant," Louisa had been tarred with the same brush.

"I don't want to learn French!" Penny said, her delicate chin jutting out with determination.

"Ah, je suis désolée," said Louisa in a tone that was not at all apologetic. *"Taisez-vous, fille stupide, et ecoutez!"*

"Miss Lymington thinks you are stupid, Penny," said Milly, the youngest. Her ears were sharp, and somehow the nine-year-old was mastering all of Louisa's lessons far faster than her two elder sisters.

Penny began to wail at that. She had no more ability to keep her emotions under lock and key than did a hungry infant. "Not only does Uncle Bertie torment us by trapping us in the wilds of Yorkshire, but he has found us the harshest of all jailers to belittle us under the guise of education. I doubt that even Emily St. Aubert had to deal with such perfidious cruelty."

Louisa rolled her eyes. Miss Trafford might have read *The Mysteries of Udolpho,* but she clearly had no idea what it really meant to have a villainous uncle. "Now Ginny," she said, ignoring Penny's outburst. "Repeat after me: *Je m'appelle Ginevra.*"

Ginny screwed up her face to attempt the intimidating syllables. "*Jum apple Ginevra.*"

Louisa tried to conceal her distaste at such an unfortunate accent. Miss Ginevra Trafford might not be as refractory as her sister, but she clearly had no ear for imitation. "A valiant attempt," Louisa managed to say. It was not an altogether truthful statement, but the new governess was determined to reward painstaking efforts over emotional outbursts.

At least Milly was on her way to becoming a proficient. "*Je m'appelle Camilla,*" she said without being prompted. "*Comment allez-vous?*"

"*Je vais bien,*" responded Louisa. *I am doing well.* But was she doing well? She had been a governess for four weeks and already the activity grated on her like a door with rusty hinges. Could she sustain such a position for nearly a year before coming into her majority? At least there was no Mr. Digby at Barrowby Park, but dealing with a spoiled minx like Penelope Trafford was almost as infuriating.

Louisa pasted on a false smile. "Your turn, Penny: *Je m'appelle Penelope.*"

"No," said Penny, crossing her arms again. "I won't say it. And neither would Admiral Nelson if he were here."

"Admiral Nelson died at Trafalgar," remarked Milly helpfully.

"All the more reason for him not to say it," retorted Penny.

"Of course he wouldn't say it," said Louisa sharply. "He would say: *Je m'appelle Horatio Nelson.* But *you* will say *Je m'appelle Penelope,* or I shall tell Cook that you won't be joining us for tea."

"What?" gasped Penny. "You wouldn't dare. I shall tell Uncle Bertie that you mean to starve me into submission to your tyrannical whims." The dark-haired girl pulled herself up to her full height as she glared at Louisa, clearly piqued that her governess was still five inches taller than her.

"Tell him whatever you want," said Louisa, "but you *will* say—"

The opening door interrupted that ultimatum. Lord Kendall's aristocratic face peeked inside the schoolroom. "Miss Lymington," he said in sombre tones, before Penny could utter her complaint, "might I have a word downstairs in my study?"

"Oh, of course," said Louisa, adding a curtsy once again as an afterthought. *What on earth could he want?* She hoped Lord Kendall had nothing to criticise in her pedagogical methods, for she did not think her patience could stand any critique. If her need to avoid London had not been so great, she would have packed her trunk already and boarded the mail coach once again. But as things were, she had better bide her time and find out what Lord Kendall had to tell her.

Chapter Eight

Blackmail

"Have a seat, Lady Louisa." The Earl of Kendall gestured to a chair positioned near his desk.

Louisa lifted the hem of her skirts and sat down. No sooner had her weight left her slippers than a feeling of imminent doom came over her.

What was that he called you?

"I see you don't deny it."

"Pardon me, my lord, but my name is *Miss* Lymington—"

"Lady Louisa Lymington, daughter of the late Duke of Warrenton."

Louisa's full lips set into a straight line.

How did he discover your identity?

"Lymington is a common name—"

"Not that common." He cast her a look of sympathy. "You must realise that I am much of an age with your parents and that I knew your mother."

"But I look nothing like her!"

"In colouring perhaps, but there is something about the eyes. They sparkle when you speak French. And that tone of voice is unmistakable."

Louisa's right slipper began to tap anxiously against the floor. "Well, now that you know, what do you mean to do about it?"

Lord Kendall raked a hand through his silver-streaked black hair. "First of all, I mean to ask some questions. Why masquerade as a governess?"

"It's not a masquerade," said Louisa stiffly. "I am eminently qualified to be a governess, and I believe your nieces are benefiting greatly from my instruction."

"I'm certain they are," said Lord Kendall dryly. "Or at least, two of them are. But I don't suppose your uncle knows that you've undertaken the position." He paused. "Well? Does he?"

"No." Louisa had no intention of saying anything further. Just because he had been perspicacious enough to ferret out her identity did not mean that the Earl of Kendall needed to know everything about her affairs.

The earl reached for a stack of stationery on the desk. "Then I had better write to him and apprise him of the matter."

"No!" said Louisa. She fixed a steely eye on him as if he were one of her charges instead of her employer. "You will do no such thing."

"I daresay he's ill with worry. *I* would be if one of my nieces had disappeared."

"Yes, well, my uncle's different from you." Louisa swallowed. *That* was an understatement. "He has no sentimental attachment to me, and his sole goal is to force me to marry so he can gain control of my fortune."

"Hmm." Lord Kendall's face looked disappointed. "Perhaps you're less sensible than I gave you credit for. Is that trunk you brought with you full of Mrs. Radcliffe novels?"

No doubt he thinks you as silly as his niece Penelope.

Louisa's brown eyes sparked with fire. "I assure you, my lord, I am not exaggerating in the least."

Lord Kendall reached for his pen. "And I assure you, neither am I."

There was no help for it—he meant to notify her uncle. Something desperate must be done. Louisa leapt to her feet. "I shall tell him you compromised me."

"Pardon?" Lord Kendall's chiselled jaw fell open in shock.

Louisa leaned forward, hands on his desk as she faced him. "If you write my uncle and tell him that I'm here at Barrowby Park, I shall tell him that you've compromised me, and you'll be forced to marry me."

Lord Kendall's shoulders pulled back and his patrician nose wrinkled with disgust. "What a dreadful notion. I'm old enough to be your father. Whyever would you do such a thing?"

"Let's just say that you're a far better prospect than the husband that my uncle has picked out for me." She watched his eyes travel from the inkwell to her face. "I'm deadly serious, my lord. I *will* trap you into marriage if you betray my whereabouts."

Lord Kendall leaned back against the leather upholstery in his chair. His nostrils flared. "I don't take kindly to being blackmailed."

"Then let us pretend we never had this conversation," said Louisa. "Let us pretend that you have no idea who I am, and we can carry on as we have been doing the last several weeks."

"Can we?" Lord Kendall snorted. "You'll pardon me, Lady Louisa, but I don't exactly feel inclined to trust you. I've spent the better part of twenty years avoiding being snared into matrimony, and I don't intend to sit here at Barrowby Park waiting for the parson's noose to tighten around my neck."

"What will you do then?"

"Do? I'll leave and go to London. I've been meaning to take Penny there for the season, but we shall go early. We shall enjoy the stink of summer by the Thames, and I shall undertake to give her a little town brass before the season starts in earnest. And you, my lady, will remain here in Yorkshire, as far from my spotless reputation as possible, with Ginny and Milly to keep you busy."

Louisa pulled back from the desk in surprise. Instead of exposing her presence to her uncle, he meant to give her the exact refuge she needed. "You would trust me here alone at Barrowby Park with Ginny and Milly?"

"Of course," said Lord Kendall. He gave her a grudging grin. "You might be an unscrupulous blackmailer, but you *are* an exceptionally fine governess."

CHAPTER NINE

Lemonade

DERBYSHIRE, ENGLAND ~ AUGUST 1810

THE AUGUST MORNING STARTED like any other. Gyles worked in the rose garden till the noon sun had fully risen, trying to get his outside chores completed before the heat of the day when he would go inside and make notes in his journal. He was experimenting with a new sort of irrigation line to keep the roses watered in the summer drought, and just yesterday, he had trained Archie Garrick on how to use the hoses. The lad was persistent if he was anything, and Gyles had taken pity on the spotty faced boy and given him some employment.

Nut-brown from a summer of outdoor activity, Gyles was cleaning up clippings of leaves and branches from the garden pathways when a charming faerie figure appeared before him. It was a petite young lady, with delicate features, dark black curls, and blue eyes as bright as cut sapphires.

"If you please, sir," said the girl said in breathless tones. "I am looking for a place to hide. My evil guardian is in hot pursuit, and I *cannot* be found by him."

Gyles stared. The sylph-like stranger was a vision of loveliness, made all the more beautiful by the garden surrounding her. He had never seen such a thing, unless maybe in a Lawrence painting in a London gallery...or in a walled garden at Carlton House four years ago. "Of course, miss. There's a pavilion in the rear of the garden where you can take shelter."

The young lady followed Gyles back through the rose garden until they came to the shade of the stone pavilion. Gyles recalled that he had entered a pavilion once before in a rose garden with a young lady far different than this one. That young lady had also needed assistance but had hidden her distress more carefully.

The dark-haired faerie, who introduced herself as Penelope Trafford, poured out a story of tragedy and terror fit for the London stage. Her parents had been killed in a carriage accident, and she and her sisters had been forced into the wardship of her uncaring uncle. Now, the villain had separated her from her beloved Ginny and Milly and was bringing her to London to compel her into matrimony with someone as cruel and callous as himself.

While she was speaking, Garrick came out to the pavilion bearing a pitcher of lemonade with two glasses on the tray. Clearly, Gyles' mother was aware that he had a visitor in the garden and was hoping to promote the acquaintance. Gyles almost rolled his eyes as the butler served them each a glass of the cold beverage and then hurriedly departed the way he had come.

As Miss Trafford's story continued, Gyles' breast began to swell with sympathy for the young lady. To be imposed upon and taken advantage of in such a way—her uncle sounded truly villainous! Indeed, Miss Trafford's description of him beggared belief. Her uncle was as unyielding as a customs agent, as formidable as a barrister for the Crown, and as cruel as a Barbary pirate. He offered her a second glass of lemonade, and she gulped it down gratefully. "If there is anything I can do to assist you, Miss Trafford, you have only to name it—"

"Penelope Trafford!" A new voice boomed like a timpani across the garden paths and into the pavilion.

The young lady shrieked, jumped up from her chair, and darted around the table to hide behind Gyles' shoulder. The tall gentleman entering the pavilion had the same crystalline blue eyes that the young lady possessed, and Gyles, with laudable intuition, knew that he was about to make the acquaintance of the evil uncle.

"So, you have found me at last, have you?" said Miss Trafford. "You may have fooled everyone else with your false charm, but I see through it to the cold-hearted monster that you are. I refuse to be used for your own selfish purposes. Mark my words, uncle, your time of tyranny is coming to an end."

Gyles could see his mother close behind the stranger, looking a little flushed from the sun in the garden. She seemed more out of breath than alarmed, but even so, Gyles ordered the man to stand back. "Your niece has told me of the wrongs done to her, and I'll not let you take her from this place."

The gentleman sighed. "Mr. Audeley, I am not sure what tales my ward has been telling you, but let me assure you that her safety and wellbeing are very much my concern." It was a reasonable statement, far too dull for the Drury Lane tale Miss Trafford had been drumming up. But wolfish uncles could wear sheep's clothing too. Gyles watched as Miss Trafford came out from her position behind his shoulder to stand her ground in front of her uncle. He knew little of who was in the right in this situation, but a lady who cried ill-treatment deserved to be believed until events proved otherwise.

"Perhaps we might all sit down and discuss this in a civilised manner," said Gyles' mother. Reluctantly, the embattled foursome sunk into the chairs around the table. Gyles wished that there were more lemonade to go around, for this promised to be a lengthy conversation.

At his mother's prompting, Miss Trafford repeated the story that she had already shared with him, how her uncle, Lord Kendall, had become her guardian after the tragedy of her parents' death, and how he was forcibly removing her to London away from her two sisters. She begged Gyles to stop her uncle from spiriting her away to the metropolis. Much to Lord Kendall's disgust, Gyles assured her that he would stand by her.

As the air continued to grow warmer, they retired to the drawing room inside the house to continue the debate. Lord Kendall insisted on his right to remove his ward that very afternoon. Miss Trafford cast Gyles such a *speaking* look, that he felt obliged, once again, to intervene. "I shan't let her go to London all alone with you."

"You really think I would allow a young pup like you to trail after us?" Lord Kendall's voice was as inflexible as iron, but, unlike Gyles' father, he still retained a modicum of good humour when he was annoyed.

"But that's a simply marvellous idea," said Miss Trafford. "Why, if Mrs. Audeley and Gyles—that is to say, *Mr.* Audeley—were to go to London too, then I should feel ever so much safer and more comfortable." She cast a look of utter devotion at Gyles.

It was a warmer sort of emotion than Gyles cared to awaken, but still, it made him feel as if he ought to earn that devotion with some other mettle than words. "We have been talking about taking a house in London for the season."

"We have?" said his mother, her face a perfect picture of shock beneath her lace cap. "But what about your roses?"

"Garrick's nephew can water and prune them." God willing, Archie was obedient enough to stick to a very strict list of instructions. Perhaps Gyles could post back to Derbyshire every few weeks to check on matters and ensure that his instructions were being carried out—

"But my dear! What about the Sweet-Scented China Rose which should bloom for the very first time this summer?"

Gyles took a deep breath. Here it was. The supreme sacrifice that chivalry demanded. "I shall bring it with us," he said, hoping that it would transplant successfully into an earthenware pot. He remembered that the prince's gardener at Carlton House had kept all the roses in planters—but it was warm weather to be displacing his prize rose bush so haphazardly.

Miss Trafford clapped her hands with glee. "Then it's all settled. We shall travel to London together. Oh, it shall be so grand." And there it was again—that supreme look of adoration cast in Gyles' direction.

He smiled shyly in return. Miss Trafford was certainly lovely, and her girlish dramatics were quite the opposite of the solid and sensible Miss Morrison. She was beautiful *and* she needed him.

But, at the same time, there was something in Miss Trafford's effervescent emotions that troubled Gyles a little—was beauty always this volatile? If so, the trip to London promised to be a highly unpredictable affair.

CHAPTER TEN

London

THE TRIP TO LONDON was undertaken without any mishap. Gyles, much to Miss Trafford's disappointment, elected to ride in his own carriage to keep an eye on the Sweet-Scented China Rose that he was bringing with him. He was resolved to document every step of the transplant and migration to the metropolis to see just how hardy this variety of rosebush was.

Miss Trafford had pouted a little when she saw the rosebush taking pride of place in the Audeley carriage, but her liveliness reignited itself when she discovered that Gyles' mother would accompany her and her uncle. "You must tell me all about yourself," Miss Trafford gushed, her words wafting out the Kendall carriage window into the warm air, "and about your son too."

Gyles found himself breathing a sigh of relief in the quiet of his own carriage. It was all well and good to rescue a damsel in distress, but one never considered how unpleasant it might be to have to accompany the damsel across half the length of

England. Miss Trafford had exactly the qualities that Miss Morrison lacked—beauty, imagination, enthusiasm—but none of the ones that made Miss Morrison so supremely sensible. If only there could be a perfect blend of the two women. Gyles grinned to himself at the thought of grafting virtues onto humans in the same manner as new varieties were grafted onto rose stems.

When they arrived in London, the Audeleys stayed at a hotel until they could find more permanent lodgings. Their solicitor did not think it possible to let a house near Mayfair for the price Mrs. Audeley wanted to pay, but Lord Kendall, with the canny knowledge of a London local, discovered a house for let that was perfect for their needs and not too far from his own home in Grosvenor Square.

The one thing the house lacked was any sort of garden, but Lord Kendall obligingly allowed Gyles to plant the rosebush in the courtyard behind Kendall House—a fitting gesture since the earl was, in a sense, responsible for uprooting the Audeleys from Derbyshire. It was a little spot of beauty in a sea of stone and brick. For the first week, all seemed well, but as the late summer heat continued, the bush began to look a little bedraggled. One afternoon, after a thorough inspection, Gyles could see that the sepals on one of the buds had grown most alarmingly yellow.

"I don't know what to do with it," he said morosely. "The whole bush may be going into shock. I think I must call on Sir Abraham Hume."

His mother nodded. "It is high time you met the man after corresponding with him for so many years. You must take the carriage, and I can see if Lord Kendall will give Penelope and me the use of his. Shall you mind, then, if I go shopping with Penelope without you?"

"Certainly not," said Gyles, his mind on far more important matters than Penelope Trafford. His mother sent him a look of surprise. Clearly, she was wondering why he had not been more attentive to the melodramatic maiden who had prompted their visit to London. He decided to convey his opinion on the matter in no uncertain terms. "How pleasant it is for Lord Kendall to take on the task of escorting you ladies so I shall not be taxed with it."

"That is not very gallant," protested his mother. "I daresay Penelope would be quite put out if she learned you were only happy to protect her from her guardian when milliner's shops are not involved."

"Oh, do you think I ought to come then?" Gyles began to worry that his trip to visit Sir Abraham must be postponed. "I must confess, on our trip here, Lord Kendall lulled me into thinking that he is not as terrible as Miss Trafford describes. But she says his affability is all a front and that I must not be taken in. If you think my presence is required—"

"No, no," said his mother. "You may tend to your rosebush. I have everything well in hand."

Sir Abraham Hume lived in the fashionable part of town. As a member of Parliament, he had arrived in town early this year. Rather than waiting till after Christmas, Parliament planned to convene in the autumn months to examine the fitness of His Majesty for rule and to discuss whether a Regency with Prince George at the helm might be for the best during these turbulent times. If this war with France were to ever end, a firmer hand was needed. England could not be ruled by insanity if Napoleon was to be one day defeated.

With the summer sun still holding sway, however, Parliament had not yet opened its doors, and apparently, Sir Abraham's political duties still left time for visitors of the botanical variety. Gyles waited only a few minutes in the portrait-clad entryway before he was admitted to Sir Abraham's study. He saw a lean old fellow with a fringe of flyaway white hair along the sides of his balding head.

"Audeley!" the baronet said, bounding up from his desk with enthusiasm. "You're younger than I expected."

Gyles accepted the statement without demur. It *was* unusual for a man of three and twenty to be so devoted to rosarian pursuits. Sir Abraham was not the first to remark upon it.

"What can I do for you? How is that Sweet-Scented China Rose faring?"

"That's what I want to talk to you about," said Gyles, fingering the brim of his beaver. "It hasn't bloomed yet. I recently transplanted it to bring to London with me—"

"Oh dear! A little warm for transplanting."

"Yes, but the trip was unavoidable, and there was no one to care for it in my absence." Sir Abraham, no doubt, had a whole team of gardeners to tend his succession houses in Hertfordshire, but Garrick's nephew was hardly a worthy substitute for a matter of this delicacy. "The foliage is beginning to yellow."

"Hmm..." Sir Abraham sank down into the chair at the desk once again and motioned for Gyles to do the same in one of the armchairs across from him. "There are two conditions that come to mind that would result in yellowing of foliage."

A protracted conversation followed in which Sir Abraham asked pointed questions about the quality of the soil the rosebush had been placed in and the length of time it took for water to absorb at the base of the bush. "There's your answer," he said. "Drainage. Very poor where you have it." He began to discuss ways of ameliorating the soil with rough sand and pebbles. "In some ways, we have it very difficult in our climate. Poor soil, and not enough sun to truly bring out the best in our flowers. Malmaison, on the other hand, that's where real strides can be made with these cultivars from the east."

"Malmaison—in France?"

"Just so. The former empress Josephine lives there. It's a boon to mankind that Napoleon divorced her this year, for now she can focus on her first love—roses!" Sir Abraham pulled out a journal that lay at the side of his desk. It was a portfolio of loose watercolours, each containing a different specimen of rose. "She has an artist working for her, documenting each variety with wonderful precision." He gestured to a bicoloured specimen. "Look here! Have you ever seen the like?"

Gyles took up the watercolour with almost reverent eagerness. The contrasting layers of bright pink and paler pink gleamed like the edges of a tropical shell. This artist, whoever he might be, was a master of capturing a flower in all its precision and beauty. Gyles felt a little jealous that he had never learned to draw himself. His own rosarian notes would be greatly enhanced with watercolours of this kind.

"Have you been to Malmaison, sir?"

"No. More's the pity." Sir Abraham sighed and leafed through the portfolio for another painted piece to show his guest. "I should like to someday, but with that blasted Bonaparte warmongering his way across Europe, I don't know when it will be safe to travel."

***

The Audeleys initially had little acquaintance in London besides Mrs. Audeley's old friends the Haverstalls, but their connection with Lord Kendall soon yielded a wider social circle. Gyles was introduced to two bachelor gentlemen—Mr. Tavinstock and Mr. Heller—who invited him to their club, their haberdasher, and their other haunts about town.

On one occasion, he and his mother rode out in Mr. Tavinstock's barouche through Hyde Park. The affable fellow, with his crisply starched cravat and crisply pomaded hair, was acquainted with all the world. By the time they had gone halfway around the Ring, Gyles' head was ringing with the number of introductions and well wishes from stopping carriages and riders. His mother, however, seemed particularly pleased with their conquest of the ton, and so Gyles pasted on a pleasant smile and pretended that he was as eager as she to make the acquaintance of every baronet and his brother.

"Warrenton and Digby are bearing down on us," said Mr. Heller. Gyles looked over his shoulder and saw two more unknown men approaching on horseback. They slowed their mounts and reined in at the side of the barouche. "Mr. Tavinstock, Mr. Heller," said the taller of the two men, nodding at their companions in the barouche. The man's voice was as firm as his shoulders, and Gyles suspected that the fellow was nearly the same age as his mother. Although Gyles was no connoisseur of clothing, he could tell the gentleman was immaculately attired in one of those suits from Wembley's or Weston's that Lord Kendall also wore.

The second rider was a marked contrast to his friend. Short and rotund, he seemed ill at ease on a horse and equally ill at ease in the area of fashion. Gyles grimaced at the sight of the second man's green paisley waistcoat which did not sort well at all with his bilious complexion.

"Mrs. Audeley," said Mr. Heller, "may I present his grace, the Duke of Warrenton. And beside him, Mr. Solomon Digby."

"I am pleased to meet you both. And this is my son, Mr. Gyles Audeley."

"You must be new to London, Mrs. Audeley," the Duke of Warrenton said, his nostrils flaring as he spoke. Gyles did not particularly like the man's appraising look as he took in his mother's appearance. "I would have remembered seeing you before."

"Yes, we are but newly arrived from Derbyshire."

"And did *Mr.* Audeley accompany you from Derbyshire?" Mr. Digby asked gruffly. It was a personal question to demand of someone so recent an acquaintance.

"I am a widow, Mr. Digby." Gyles' mother spoke with quiet dignity.

"Are you now?" replied Mr. Digby. His heavily lidded eyes gave an insinuating look, and Gyles began to dislike the fellow immensely. One never thinks of one's parents as attractive, and Gyles had never considered that his mild-mannered mother would awaken such interest in the metropolis.

"I say, your grace," interrupted Mr. Tavinstock, steering the conversation off in a new direction. "We've all been waiting to catch sight of the Incomparable from last season. Where has Lady Louisa been hiding herself?"

The Duke of Warrenton did not seem to welcome the question. "You must be patient, Mr. Tavinstock," he said curtly. "The season hasn't even begun. I daresay you'll see my niece soon enough."

"The trick is," drawled Mr. Heller, "to see her before she's gone and engaged herself to some other fellow. I wouldn't expect a girl that pretty to last two seasons on the marriage mart."

"You're right about that," said Mr. Digby with a smug smile. "I'll lay you a monkey that Lady Louisa has a different surname next time you see her."

"I hope you are misinformed, Mr. Digby," said Mr. Tavinstock. "Young Audeley here has not even had the pleasure of catching a single glimpse of her. How cruel if she were to be spirited away over the summer."

Gyles lifted a hand in protest. As much as he appreciated beauty, he had no interest in pursuing some unknown Incomparable.

"Nonsense," said the Duke of Warrenton. "No one has spirited anyone away. Shall we continue our ride, Digby?" The duke lifted his hand to his beaver and tipped it towards the barouche. "Charmed to have made your acquaintance, Mrs. Audeley. I shall call on you, if I may."

"Of course," said Mrs. Audeley, in a tone that was—in Gyles' opinion—far more friendly than the duke and his uncouth friend deserved. The Duke of Warrenton and the Earl of Kendall were six of one and half a dozen of the other in the eyes of the world, but somehow, Gyles trusted Lord Kendall far more than he did the duke when it came to visiting his mother.

CHAPTER ELEVEN

Summons

YORKSHIRE, ENGLAND ~ SEPTEMBER 1810

"Curve your fingers, Milly," said Louisa, tapping time on her knee as the girl played on the pianoforte. "And you must stretch your thumb a little farther to reach the E. Since your hands are small, they must work harder to master Mozart."

With Penelope and Lord Kendall gone to the metropolis, lessons had become far simpler. Ginny placidly accepted every task given to her, and talented little Milly thrived in being pushed to excel. Louisa discovered that by taking a little time to herself to walk the grounds each morning, she then retained the patience to tutor the two girls all day in mathematics, music, drawing, French, and Italian. Indeed, she was almost *enjoying* the task, something she had never expected when she had answered the advertisement at Barrowby Park.

"Miss Lymington, how long did it take *you* to master Mozart?" asked Milly.

"One doesn't ever, truly. I'm still mastering him. But here, let me show you how this piece should sound."

Milly slid over on the bench, and Louisa, sitting down, set fingers to keys in a rapid crescendo leading to the final cadence. "*Brava!*" said Milly. It was strange to play the pianoforte for someone so appreciative. It was true that her talents had been lauded when she played at musicales during the season, but Milly's awed applause was far more intimate than the fawning approval of a room full of sycophantic suitors.

"You are marvellous, Miss Lymington."

"And so shall you be, someday soon." Uncomfortable with the adulation, Louisa stood up from the bench to let Milly practise and walked to the other side of the drawing room to examine Ginny's stitchery.

"This is very neat."

"Yes," said Ginny. Her features were broader than her sister's, and she looked up from her needlework with a cheerful gleam in her blue eyes. "I may be slow, but I can stitch a satisfactory chain of daisies."

"You think you are slow?"

"Haven't you noticed?" There was a tone of disbelief in Ginny's voice. "I'm slower than Penny and Milly at *everything*. I think it's because I have such trouble making up my mind what to do when a choice presents itself. Two stitches or three stitches? Green or blue ribbon? Chip bonnet or poke bonnet?" She looked at Louisa admiringly. "*You* seem to have no trouble deciding what to do in life, Miss Lymington."

Louisa lifted an eyebrow. "Indeed. I have never been accused of indecision." She imagined that Uncle Nigel had been deploring her decisive departure for the last couple months. Had Mr. Digby demanded the return of the money her uncle had borrowed from him? What would happen when he could not repay it? Mr. Digby did not seem like the sort of man to accept a swindle without repercussions.

Louisa shook off those unpleasant thoughts and forced her mind to consider her charges once again. Milly, persistent at the pianoforte, finally played the closing measures of the rondo perfectly. "Good," said Louisa curtly. "Lord Kendall will be proud of you when he returns to Yorkshire."

"Or when we go to London," piped up Milly.

"Go to London?" Louisa's creamy brow crinkled in confusion.

"Didn't we tell you?" said Ginny, setting down her embroidery. "A letter came this morning while you were out for your walk. Uncle Bertie says we're to join him in town."

"How preposterous," said Louisa. "I fear that will greatly interrupt your progress on the pianoforte, Milly." How were the girls to travel to London on their own? And what on earth was *she* to do at Barrowby Park with her charges gone to the metropolis?

"But Uncle Bertie has an instrument at the London townhouse, and you shall be coming with us, so my lessons can continue."

"Coming with you?" Louisa's voice turned sharp. "Nonsense."

"Yes, look at the letter." Ginny rose from her seat and asked the butler to fetch the letter which had arrived earlier. The longer missive addressed to his nieces contained a note from Lord Kendall to her, a note that was as curt as it was commanding.

Miss Lymington,

The coachman has orders to leave in the morning and bring you, Ginny, and Milly to London. The enclosed itinerary contains the best stopping places and inns along the way. The girls will be pleased to arrive in time for Penny's coming-out ball. You will be happy to learn that I have obtained adequate chaperonage at the London house in the person of Mrs. Miranda Gale, a distant relative of mine, so there can be no accusations of impropriety.

Kendall

Louisa bit her lip in frustration. There was no way for her to evade these direct instructions. Unless she terminated her position as governess, she would have to travel back to the dangers of London.

And even if you terminate your position as governess, where would you go? Lord Kendall has the upper hand now.

"No more lessons today," Louisa said. "Go upstairs, girls, and pack your things." She would need to repack her own monstrous trunk, half of which was still full of fancy evening wear and hidden jewels. The plain grey dresses she had worn when mourning her father were the only pieces that she had taken out of the box, and when she returned to London, there would be even more need for her to dress unobtrusively and wear a veil with her bonnet.

Mayfair was not large. It was a distinct possibility that she would pass either Uncle Nigel or Mr. Digby on the street. If she wanted to maintain her anonymity, it would not be wise to show the face that had been proclaimed the Incomparable of the last London season.

CHAPTER TWELVE

Vauxhall

London, England ~ September 1810

Gyles sighed. If Penelope Trafford gasped and grasped his arm one more time, he thought he might lose his temper. Every single sight at Vauxhall seemed to either carry her into raptures or terrify her beyond measure. His enthusiasm for Miss Trafford's company had begun to pall, wilting like an unwatered rose in the late summer heat.

It was September now, and Lord Kendall had proposed that they visit Vauxhall since it was the last week the weather was likely to remain fair and the gardens likely to remain open. Gyles had explored this tourist attraction with his father and mother four years ago and seen the lovely fairy grove of lanterns by night. This time, however, Gyles' party visited Vauxhall in the afternoon as Lord Kendall did not think it proper for Miss Trafford to dine and dance under the moon until she had officially come out at her own ball.

Without the romance of evening attached to it, Gyles could see the strange mix of tawdriness and sophistication which defined the gardens. The walkways were laid out neatly in symmetrical patterns. Sprinkled throughout were various painted pavilions, empty now but set up for the orchestras that would perform later in the evening. In the open areas, jugglers and acrobats exercised their limbs for the benefit of perambulating tourists. Lord Kendall was adept at directing them past the more unsavoury denizens of Vauxhall, an assortment of pickpockets and prostitutes who called the pleasure gardens home. His chaperonage was so skilled that Miss Trafford, who surely would have asked questions about anything she did not understand, was not even aware of the bits of muslin lurking in the corners.

Over the past month, Gyles had developed a considerable respect for the earl. He was nothing like the villain that Penny had painted him, and his nieces needed no protection from him. The eldest Miss Trafford, as Gyles had come to know all too well, varnished her stories with a great deal of colour that was not always true to life. Some men might find her naive exuberance and high-strung histrionics charming. Gyles was beginning to find them exhausting.

His mother, Mrs. Audeley, had taken the motherless girl under her wing and currently spent every afternoon at Kendall House helping with the preparations for Penelope's ball. When he was not requisitioned to escort Penelope to various amusements, Gyles amused himself by visiting the many public gardens throughout London and continuing his writing on the varieties of roses he encountered. Today, however, he had agreed to visit Vauxhall and was bearing the brunt of Penelope's excitement.

"Will we see the Cascade?" she demanded, looking about for the enormous mechanical waterfall which was one of the main features of the place.

"No," said Lord Kendall. "They only set it in motion once night falls. It runs in time with the fireworks."

"Oh," said Penelope with a pout, having already forgotten her delight at the painted ceiling of the rotunda and her gleeful terror at the tower of acrobats three men tall. "Then why did we even come?"

"The balloon ascension is the chief attraction in the afternoons," said Gyles, pointing to where the ascension was shortly to take place. As a crowd began to form, two men climbed into the woven basket that was tied down by ropes and stakes while above them hundreds of yards of silk billowed in the wind and bulged with air.

Gyles felt Miss Trafford grab his arm again. "Good heavens! I would never, for all the world, climb into that basket. You cannot make me do it."

"My dear Penny," said the longsuffering Lord Kendall, "no one is attempting to make you do so. We've merely come to *watch* the ascension."

The balloon, still tethered by ropes, began to lift before their eyes. Penny gave a shriek of excited terror and clutched Gyles so tightly that he began to wonder if his arm would be returned to him unscathed. Ten minutes aloft and then it was all over. The men descended to earth again, and Penelope repeated her ultimatum that no one could make her do such a thing. Not even Mrs. Radcliffe's heroines had been subjected to such torment.

"You'd never expect it of me, would you, Mr. Audeley?" Her brilliant blue eyes looked at him beseechingly.

"Of course not, Miss Trafford," said Gyles, trying to keep the irritation out of his voice. By this point, his expectations of Penelope were very low indeed. He was beginning to think that Miss Morrison with her seed drills and crop rotation and useful felines was far better company.

Following the ascension, Lord Kendall seemed eager to return to the house, so Gyles and Penelope returned to the carriage and spent a less dramatic ride back to Mayfair discussing the palaces and pedestrians they passed along the town streets. When they reached Kendall House, another sight greeted them outside the front door.

"Uncle Bertie, isn't that your second carriage?" asked Penny.

"Why, so it is!" said Lord Kendall. "You're in for another surprise today, Penny. Come inside and see."

CHAPTER THIRTEEN

Meeting

ONE WOULD EXPECT THAT a trip in an earl's carriage would be far more pleasant than riding in a mail coach. However, they had gone no farther than Doncaster, to the first inn on Lord Kendall's list, when Louisa encountered the grossest impertinence.

Upon entering the rooms assigned to them, Louisa discovered that they were adorned with musty bedclothes and skittering six-legged creatures. Disgusted, she went to speak with the innkeeper about new accommodations. The regular innkeeper was sick abed, and his son mistook Louisa, in her drab dress, for a maid. Apparently, the rascally fellow was of the mind that maids deserved less deference than fine ladies, for when she asked for cleaner accommodations for the Miss Traffords and herself, he responded with a saucy smirk and a pinch on her derriere.

The impudence was unforgivable! Louisa's velvety brown eyes turned to purple flame, and as Ginny and Milly descended the stairs, they witnessed their governess give the man a dressing down that spared neither his manners, intellect, nor appearance. The innkeeper's son began to curse at her and accused her of being "no better than she ought t'be." Ginny grabbed hold of Louisa's arm in fright, and Milly went running to tell the coachman that they'd not be staying in Doncaster after all.

The ladies travelled several miles farther down the road before they found an inn that Louisa deemed acceptable. Although it was not an approved stopping place on Lord Kendall's itinerary, the innkeeper provided them with a private parlour in which to dine and beds free from vermin. Milly and Ginny shared a room while Louisa kept to her own bed in the room next door. She could hear the girls giggling long after the candle had been extinguished. She wondered that they could be in such charity with each other after such a long day of travel. Perhaps the companionship of a sister made up for the minor annoyances of life?

Or perhaps you're simply growing maudlin as an old grandmother. You've done well enough with just yourself for companion. And you'll need to keep your wits about you and keep your own counsel once this carriage arrives in Mr. Digby's hometown.

On the afternoon of the third day, they arrived in London. The coachman deposited them at the door of a fine-looking townhouse—although not so grand as the Warrenton establishment—and Louisa hurried her charges inside before she should be seen on the street.

Lord Kendall was not home to greet them. A hunched older woman, very hard of hearing, began to question their appearance. Louisa suspected this lady was the Mrs. Gale whom Lord Kendall had engaged as a chaperone, but Ginny and Milly did not recognise her and worried that they'd been taken to the wrong townhouse.

"Impossible," said Louisa dryly. "The driver is your uncle's own coachman and would not have deposited us at a strange abode."

A pretty, middle-aged woman descended on them from the drawing room, looking almost as if she were the mistress of the place. Perhaps *this* was Mrs. Gale?

Before the situation could be untangled, the front door burst open, revealing the eldest Miss Trafford, Lord Kendall, and an unknown gentleman. Penelope went into raptures over the arrival of her sisters, Milly was hoisted up in a bearhug in her uncle's arms, and in the flurry of greetings, it was some time before the earl could introduce the unknown members of the party.

Apparently, the hunched old woman who was now clinging for support to the arm of the earl's secretary, was the requisite chaperone, Mrs. Gale. That pitiful creature would protect the earl's reputation with Louisa in the house.

The pretty middle-aged lady with dark hair was not a chaperone at all, but a "friend of the family." Lord Kendall introduced her as Mrs. Audeley. There was such a tone of gentle pride in his voice that Louisa looked the woman over sharply. Clearly, she meant something to the earl. Was this why he had been so horrified at the thought of Louisa entrapping him?

"And this," said Lord Kendall, drawing attention to the young man who had entered the door behind him, "is Mrs. Audeley's son, Gyles."

Louisa's heart tripped over itself like an inexperienced rider trying to take a hedge at a gallop. What name had he said? Gyles? It was a name so lacking in popularity that she had not heard it again since her flight from Carlton House. But surely, there were more Gyles in England than just the one?

Her eyes darted to the gentleman's face. He was a little taller, a little tanner, and a little broader than she remembered him—but he was still, unmistakably, the chivalrous rosarian from four years ago at Carlton House.

He was looking at her, a puzzled furrow on his brow, as if that same memory were lurking beneath the surface of his mind and about to leap forth like a lake trout. Louisa bowed her head, trying to shield her face. She had often wondered if she would meet the presumptuous trespasser again. Wondered, and waited, and—if she were honest with herself—hoped. But to greet him now would awaken comment that she could ill afford. She began to thank God that the mysterious Gyles had never asked for her name.

But did he recognise the coat-of-arms on your carriage at Carlton House? If so, then he knows exactly who you are. If he recognises your face, can you count on his discretion as much as Lord Kendall's? You have nothing with which to blackmail Gyles Audeley....

Louisa swallowed and edged along the wall, trying to look inconspicuous. She must keep away from him at all costs. Now that she was back in London, her uncle was only a stone's throw away. It was more important than ever that she remain incognito if she were to keep her freedom.

"Ginny, Milly, what a delightful surprise this is!" said Lord Kendall, his tone devoid of any concern for the impossible position in which he had placed Louisa. "I did not expect you till tomorrow."

"Miss Lymington did not like the look of the first inn you had arranged," said Ginny. "So we travelled on for several hours after that to find another one and got ahead of schedule."

"Did not like the look of the inn," repeated Lord Kendall incredulously. Clearly, he thought that his itinerary had been infallible. "Pray, what was wrong with it, Miss Lymington?"

Louisa had a tart response ready on her tongue, but she tempered it in favour of escaping notice. The less attention the better. "The sheets were insufficiently aired. And the manners of the innkeeper left something to be desired."

Milly, that precocious little pest, leaned in to whisper loudly in her uncle's ear. "He pinched Miss Lymington. On the bottom!"

Louisa refused to look up from the floor, but she felt Gyles Audeley's eyes on her and sensed the waves of indignation radiating from him. He had always been a *preux chevalier,* as her mother would have called him. *A gallant knight.* But that was the last thing she needed now when discretion was the better part of valour.

Lord Kendall attempted to smooth things over. "I apologise for the indignity you suffered, Miss Lymington. I can only hope that the second inn you found was more to your satisfaction."

"It was, your lordship." Louisa's face tightened and she glared at the earl. None of the journey was to her satisfaction, but she must make the best of it.

The eldest Miss Trafford began to giggle at the obvious awkwardness of the situation. From the corner of her eye, Louisa saw the girl reach for Gyles and wrap her own arm squarely around his. Startled, Gyles looked down at Miss Trafford. Louisa was sophisticated enough to know that Penny had seen him staring at the governess and was now proclaiming her own prior claim. Could the silly little chit be jealous of her?

Lord Kendall cleared his throat. "Penny, could you please see the girls and Miss Lymington to their rooms and help unpack their things? And Miss Lymington, perhaps you would grant me the favour of your company in my study later. I have questions about my wards' progress since last I saw them."

Louisa met the earl's stare with hauteur until she was forced to nod and drop a grudging curtsey. She could only hope that this appointment truly was about his wards' progress and not a curt command for her to return to her uncle's house. At that point, no matter his obvious predilection for Gyles' mother, she would have to make good her threat and force him into marrying her.

Mrs. Audeley chose that moment to make her *adieux*. The pretty woman seemed flustered and was holding her hand to her temple as if she had a headache coming on. Gyles disentangled himself from Miss Trafford to offer his mother an arm, and the earl and lady began to go back and forth trying to outdo each other in politeness—Lord Kendall begging them to stay for dinner and Mrs. Audeley begging off so as not to intrude on the family reunion.

Obeying her uncle without objection for once, Penny led the way up the stairs, regaling the wide-eyed Ginny with a description of all the preparations underway for her ball. Milly, who had squirmed out of her uncle's arms while he negotiated with Mrs. Audeley, skipped behind her sisters, eyeing the bannister as if it had potential for future larks. Louisa followed behind them, back straight, hands folded, eyes cast down—a useful practise for her role as an unobtrusive and unremarkable governess.

But as she ascended the stairs, Louisa realised that she was not as unobtrusive as she had hoped, for underneath his mop of chestnut curls, the brown eyes of Gyles Audeley were assessing her as keenly as if she were a rosebush in the Carlton House gardens.

Chapter Fourteen

Introduction

"DID YOU NOTICE THAT governess?" Gyles asked his mother as they rode home from Kendall House in the carriage.

"Miss Lymington?"

"Yes." Gyles pursed his lips and stared up at the ceiling of the carriage. "She was very brave to travel so far with her charges without the protection of a gentleman." He did not think Penelope Trafford would have made it more than a mile on her own—the lions they had seen at the royal menagerie several weeks ago had almost undone her and the balloon ascension had proved too much for her to even observe. His lip curled into a smile imagining how Miss Trafford would have handled an insult from an unknown innkeeper. Certainly, she would not have had the presence of mind to immediately return to the carriage and seek other accommodations. But Miss Lymington was different—different, and yet familiar. Unbidden, the name *Julia* surfaced in his thoughts. Julia Lymington....

"Indeed, she was," replied his mother, but she seemed distracted, as if her mind were still on some prior conversation with Lord Kendall rather than on the events they were discussing.

"Perhaps I shall be properly introduced to her tomorrow."

"Oh, perhaps you shall," echoed his mother. She was beginning to look very wan, and Gyles was not surprised to hear that her headache would not allow her to come down for dinner that evening.

The following day, Mrs. Audeley continued to plead illness and wished nothing more than to rest in her chamber. Gyles decided to visit Kendall House himself and examine how his Sweet-Scented China Rose was getting along. He had implemented the drainage techniques suggested by Sir Abraham, and the yellowness of the leaves and sepals was beginning to abate. It was very late in the season, however, and he began to have his doubts whether the rose bush would bloom this year.

While Gyles was at Kendall House, he saw no harm in stopping inside to greet the ladies. Little Milly was having a lesson at the pianoforte from her governess while the older sisters sat on the couch together exchanging confidences. Penny welcomed Gyles with her usual enthusiasm. "Just think, Mr. Audeley! We shall have to go to the menagerie and the other places *all over again* so that Ginny can see them too."

"Oh, is that so?" The idea of doing more sight-seeing with Penelope was enough to disconcert even the even-keeled Gyles. Fortunately, he found Ginny good-natured, agreeable, and more subdued than her elder sister. After a few minutes of conversation—in which he assured Ginny that Miss Trafford had been in *no danger whatsoever* during the balloon ascension—he asked to be introduced to their governess.

Penny's carefree attitude changed immediately, and her sparkling face fell into a sullen frown. "Mr. Audeley," she said, bringing Gyles forward to the pianoforte. "This is my *sisters'* governess, Miss Lymington."

Gyles gave a polite bow. Miss Lymington would barely look in his direction. "Pleased to meet you, Mr. Audeley. You will pardon me, but I am engaged in instructing Milly right now."

Gyles scrutinised her for a few moments longer than was polite. Her honey-gold hair was pulled back into a severe bun and her dress was as drab as an English winter. But still, the luminosity of her countenance could not be hidden or the perfect proportions of her face and figure. He attempted to strike up a conversation. "Have you instructed many pupils before?"

"Yes," she said shortly, and then leaned forward to turn the pages for Milly. "Now, see here, Milly," she continued, ignoring Gyles' presence, "you must crescendo through this section, but keep a light hand on the keys...."

Penelope looped her arm through Gyles' and led him back to the sofa on the other side of the room. "She's always frigidly civil like that. I think even Uncle Bertie is a little afraid of her. He insisted on leaving for London not four weeks after he hired her."

"No doubt she feels the need to maintain her authority as a governess and create a sense of separation." Gyles could not imagine that the governess was more than a year or two older than the eldest Miss Trafford. He also could not imagine having Penelope as a pupil—or as anything else. She would drive a man to drink after four weeks spent in her company.

"No doubt," said Penelope in a giggling whisper, "but she's not a bit of fun. I can't think why Ginny and Milly are so attached to her."

"Ah, Gyles, how are you this afternoon?" asked Lord Kendall, slapping his gloves against his opposite hand as he entered the drawing room. His beaver was on his head, and he looked as if he were just about to go out.

"Excellent," said Gyles, politely, although he was feeling less than excellent at the moment since Miss Lymington refused to say three words to him.

"And Mrs. Audeley?"

Lord Kendall's eyes brightened as he asked the question.

"My mother is feeling poorly today. A case of the megrims, I'm afraid."

"Perhaps I ought to call on her?"

"She hasn't received anyone today other than her friend Mrs. Haverstall—and that was upstairs in her chambers since she wasn't feeling up to coming downstairs."

Lord Kendall's face grew grim. "The London air must not agree with her."

Gyles did not know what to say to that. His mother had always loved being in London. He remembered her wistful face whenever his place-bound father spoke disparagingly of the metropolis.

"Perhaps when she is recovered, you both would like to accompany us to Hatchard's."

"What is that?" asked Ginny.

"London's best bookstore," said Lord Kendall with an indulgent grin. "I shall buy each of you girls a book. But no Gothic novels," he admonished Penelope with mock severity. And then, with a lighter tone, he looked over to the piano. "And that rule stands for you too, Miss Lymington."

"I'm sure such a rule is unnecessary in my case," said Miss Lymington evenly, and Gyles could tell she was exercising a good deal of control not to repay Lord Kendall's gibe in kind.

No, Miss Lymington was not the type to read Gothic literature. But somehow, Gyles suspected, if she found herself in the improbable situations of Mrs. Radcliffe, she would be quite successful in finding her way out of them without resorting to Drury Lane theatrics.

CHAPTER FIFTEEN

Hatchard's

KEEPING HER EARS OPEN as the week went on, Louisa learned that Mrs. Audeley's megrims lasted three days and then abated quite suddenly the morning the earl went to call on her. There must have been a rapprochement of some kind, for after that visit, the Audeleys were back to daily visits at Kendall House, and Louisa was put to significant exertion to avoid Gyles Audeley's constant presence.

There was an awareness between them that shimmered like the last gleam of twilight before darkness came. Louisa could not glimpse Gyles' chestnut curls without reliving the moment he had climbed the wall at Carlton House or remembering the instant he had called out to her in the stone pavilion. She could not tell if the same memories glowed in his chest beneath his plain dark waistcoat or if he had forgotten them altogether. But even if the latter were true, his brown eyes continually reached for her no matter how much she relegated herself to the outskirts of the Kendall House gatherings. He might not know her as Julia, but he certainly wanted to know her better. And that, above all things, she could not allow.

On a convenient afternoon, Lord Kendall's proposed visit to Hatchard's took place, and the party visited, browsed, and enriched the Piccadilly bookseller by the price of a half dozen novels. There was one for each of the Trafford misses and one for Mrs. Audeley herself, but Louisa declined the gift of a novel from the earl. "I am far too busy with my duties, my lord, to have time for something so frivolous."

"Doing it rather brown, Miss Lymington," said the earl, lifting an eyebrow, but he left her alone after that. Apparently, he was less interested in trying to convince an aloof governess than in finding out which volume Mrs. Audeley wished to select.

Lord Kendall had made no mention, since Louisa's arrival, of her hidden identity. Indeed, the meeting in his study had been exactly what he said it was—a discussion of his wards' progress. And Louisa had felt strangely delighted to tell him that Milly was excelling in French, Italian, drawing, and music, and that Ginny—with her more modest talents—was also proceeding as quickly as could be expected. She was beginning to hope that Lord Kendall would keep her secret indefinitely.

But what about Gyles? Did he realise who she was, and would he share that knowledge with anyone? From beneath her veil of eyelashes, Louisa observed the young man meandering through the natural history section of the store. He was too engrossed in a detailed book of botanical drawings to pay her any heed. She continued to stare, the abstracted look on his face so peacefully soothing that it was hard to pull her eyes away. Her velvet eyes lingered on his tan cheekbones and then focused on the rhythmic quality of his lips, silently murmuring the scientific nomenclature printed on the page. She watched him the way he had been watching her for the last week at Kendall House.

It was not long, however, before Louisa's better sense prevailed.

What if he should see you staring at him? Have you no shame or self-respect?

Carefully, she tore her gaze away from Gyles, as one would tear a page from a well-beloved book. Then, slipping between the freestanding shelves of books, she attempted to remove herself as far from him as possible.

But in her haste to avoid Gyles Audeley, she ended up putting *herself* on display in the window at the front of Hatchard's. Her dark bonnet covered her golden hair almost completely, but the bright window still left her feeling too exposed.

What if you should be sighted by an acquaintance passing by in the street?

Too late! With barely enough warning to react, Louisa recognised the broad shoulders of the next passer-by. It was the Duke of Warrenton, striding down Piccadilly in a trim coat and tight pantaloons. His chiselled jaw looked more careworn than she had ever seen it and his dark eyes more haunted, but Louisa's care was less for her uncle's state of mind than it was for her own safety.

No. No! Not Uncle Nigel. Not here. Has he seen you?

With a sharp intake of breath, Louisa bowed her head and stepped backwards out of the light of the window...and right into the approaching form of Gyles Audeley.

"Oh!" cried Louisa, losing her footing. As she stumbled, Gyles' hands reached out to steady her, one of them catching her elbow and the other holding fast to her waist. "Miss Lymington," he said in low tones, "are you all right?"

"Perfectly," said Louisa. She turned her head to screen her face from the window once again and discovered that her chin was almost touching Gyles' shoulder—a shoulder that was attached to an arm that was attached to a hand that was attached to her waist. "You may release me, Mr. Audeley," she said, a wave of dizziness overcoming her even as she decried her need for support.

His right hand loosened and let go of her waist, but his other hand lingered beneath her elbow. She discovered that she could not fall to the ground, even if her legs gave way, for his grip was as steady as a bannister of oak.

"Allow me to find you a chair." He guided her toward a set of armchairs in the corner of the shop.

Louisa almost objected to his solicitude, but then she realised that a chair would let her escape the overly public panorama of the shop window. Her uncle had passed by, but there was always the fear that he might finish whatever errand he was on and walk down Piccadilly again.

"You are too kind, Mr. Audeley," she said curtly as he seated her in the ruby velvet armchair.

"Something you dislike, I think." His mouth crooked into a longsuffering smile as he looked down at her from above.

Louisa flinched. "Why, what do you mean?"

"You dislike it when people are kind to you."

"I am...not accustomed to it."

Gyles' smile metamorphosed into a frown. "That is not as it should be. Miss Lymington, you must—"

Before he could say anything further, the eldest Miss Trafford entered their orbit and thrust a slim volume between them. "See here, Mr. Audeley. My uncle has purchased me a copy of *Marmion*. I hear it contains a most dreadful villain, and the heroine must suffer many trials to escape his schemes and stratagems. But it is not a novel—it is poetry, and poetry is respectable. So my uncle cannot object to it, and neither can Miss Lymington."

"How exciting," said Gyle politely.

Louisa could barely control her sense of pique at the interloping Penelope.

Why do you care so much what Gyles was about to say to you? The Audeleys mean nothing to you. Nothing at all.

"I believe that you have made it clear that I am not your governess, Miss Trafford," said Louisa, "so I have nothing to say to you on what you should or should not read."

Louisa noted with satisfaction that Penny did not know how to answer her. But the girl was clearly too jealous to leave Gyles in conversation with her "not-governess." She commandeered his assistance in retrieving another volume from a high shelf on the other side of the store. For the rest of the excursion, Louisa was left alone in the armchair, relieved that her uncle had not chosen today to buy a book at Hatchard's and perplexed that Gyles Audeley could make her lose her self-possession so completely.

CHAPTER SIXTEEN

Fencing

THE TRIP TO HATCHARD'S was followed by several more days spent planning Penelope Trafford's ball. Gyles found Miss Lymington still determined to avoid him, and indeed, she rarely put in an appearance belowstairs if the Audeleys were visiting. Eventually, however, the loose ends for the ball had all been sewn up. Gyles' mother declared that a shopping expedition was in order and that the gentlemen were *de trop*.

Lord Kendall, who would have been perfectly content to squire his nieces and Mrs. Audeley about town, could see where he was not wanted. Instead, he invited Gyles to join him in watching a bout of swordplay at Angelo's *Ecole des Armes* on Bond Street. Gyles would also have preferred to trail after the ladies—at least, he would have once he learned that a certain governess was joining the expedition—or to have remained at home so he could continue writing his chapter on soil fertilisation, but he accepted Lord Kendall's invitation with good grace.

The room at Angelo's smelled of sweat, leather, and the metallic tang of blades or blood. But at least the high ceilings held a clerestory of windows, and the place was well-lit. The school was not just for those who participated in sport but for those who liked to watch it take place. Small groups of men stood or sat at tables around the fencing floor, and the earl secured a place for Gyles and himself to sit.

Gyles did not know the first thing about fencing. His father had been more concerned with the management of his money than with fencing, shooting, hunting, or other sport. If he did not enjoy an activity himself, he would hardly waste the blunt on introducing his son to it. Even gaining a small space in the garden for two dozen rose bushes had been a difficult concession for Gyles to wring from him. As he grew into manhood, Gyles had begun to comprehend the parsimonious manner in which his father treated his family. No wonder his mother was yearning to do some long overdue shopping in London after the tight-fisted treatment to which she had been subjected.

The fencing match was between Mr. Heller and Viscount Landsdowne. Gyles was coming to appreciate Mr. Heller as a fledgling friend, but the viscount was unknown to him. The two men seemed evenly matched—but then, Gyles was ignorant of what constituted real skill. When Viscount Landsdowne pricked Mr. Heller with the tip of his foil, the room erupted in a roar of applause and then quieted again as the match continued in earnest.

Lord Kendall, eyes on the fencing floor, kept up a steady flow of conversation with Gyles. He seemed curious about Gyles' parents, and the young man found himself sharing details about his mother and father that he had never shared with anyone. As they talked, a large fellow with a bright mauve waistcoat, entered the salon and marched his way across the corner of the fencing floor until he paused in front of their table. "Careful, Digby," said the earl. "You're blocking our view of the match."

Gyles recalled meeting the fellow, on horseback in the Duke of Warrenton's company in Hyde Park. He would never have recalled the man's name, but apparently Lord Kendall was familiar with him.

"Oh, pardon me," said Mr. Digby, his accent betraying his lower-class origins. He removed his beaver and scratched the rim of his balding head. "Hello, Kendall. Audeley."

Apparently, Mr. Digby remembered *his* name.

"I'm surprised to see you here," said Lord Kendall. "Angelo's is hardly your typical tea and biscuits."

Gyles smiled at that metaphor. One could readily imagine the sleek Earl of Kendall stripping down to his shirtsleeves for a round of sabre strokes, but the ponderous physique of Solomon Digby would have been more at home at a dining table than on a fencing floor.

"I need some information," said Mr. Digby with a grunt. "There's a gel promised to me, but her guardian keeps putting me off. Haven't seen hide nor hair of her since midsummer. Where's she got to, I'm wondering? Thought I'd get to a watering spot and hear the latest gossip."

Gyles was confused. "You speak as if this girl were a horse." Who would promise any girl to such a lout?

"Oh, stap me, certainly not. This one's a prime filly, high-mettled, not quite broken to harness."

Gyles grimaced, ready for the conversation to be over. He could not imagine using such coarse verbiage to describe any of the ladies of his acquaintance.

"Does this filly have a name?" Lord Kendall raised an eyebrow.

Digby took on a sly look. He leaned in to whisper. "It's Lady Louisa, the Duke of Warrenton's niece. Has a hundred thousand pounds from her mother's side."

It was a tidy sum. Had he been interested in heiresses, Gyles would have perked up an ear. But the thought of seeking out a lady for her monetary value had never occurred to him.

"No wonder you're looking for her," said Lord Kendall.

"Oh, she has other qualities as well." Digby spent the next few moments describing the woman's figure in such keen detail that Gyles almost told the lascivious old fellow to stow it or shove off. But as much as he detested such conversation, he could not help comparing the bawdy description to the appearance of the remarkable woman who consumed most of his thoughts each day with her honey-gold hair, violet-brown eyes, and heart-shaped face. Could they possibly be one and the same? Could Miss Lymington be both his Julia from Carlton House *and* the niece to the Duke of Warrenton?

"And so Warrenton's putting you off, is he?" interrupted Lord Kendall. "What does he say?"

"He says she's visiting family in a remote location. Claims she'll be back in London at the start of the season."

"Then you must just be patient, man," said the earl. "That is, if you trust Warrenton." Mr. Digby frowned, that little nudge from the earl causing the wheels in his head to begin turning.

Gyles' mind was also spinning. He had seen Warrenton in Hyde Park astride a horse, but he would give a good deal to see him in his carriage—and to see the coat-of-arms that was painted on the door. After his last trip to London, he had spent months regretting his stupid failure to ask the unknown Julia her name, but it seemed that Providence had both thrown her back into his path and given him another chance to identify her.

The room erupted in applause again as the viscount landed another good hit on Mr. Heller's lower left ribs. Lord Kendall rose from his chair to applaud and Gyles followed suit.

Viscount Landsdowne had won. Lord Kendall moved to congratulate him while Gyles went to exchange a few words with Mr. Heller.

"A good effort," he proclaimed, speaking more from friendship than knowledge.

"Not fast enough by far," said Mr. Heller, mopping the sweat from his face with a cloth. "Landsdowne's quick as the devil with his parries. Thought I had him cornered a minute ago, but he set me back on my toes soon enough." He gave Gyles a rueful smile. "You here with Kendall?"

"Yes," said Gyles, looking over to where the earl was deep in conversation with Viscount Landsdowne.

"Hmm, makes sense. Soon to be your father, eh?"

"I beg your pardon?" Gyles turned back to Mr. Heller in surprise.

"Oh," said Mr. Heller, colouring. "Just a rumour I heard. Pay no attention to me. Never get things right side up, at least, that's what Tavinstock tells me."

Gyles cleared his throat and changed the subject. But inside, his mind travelled back to the earlier conversation with Mr. Digby. Had *he* got things right side up? Or was Miss Lymington just who she said she was—a governess who looked remarkably like someone he had once met?

CHAPTER SEVENTEEN

Shopping

Louisa agreed to accompany the Trafford sisters on their shopping trip, but only after it was determined that the gentlemen would not be included. She could not risk further proximity to Gyles Audeley—not after the way he had looked at her so searchingly in Hatchard's.

Once again, she wore a close-fitting bonnet that would screen her face, and then keeping quiet as befit a governess, she let the chatter of her charges carry her all the way to Pall Mall. Mrs. Audeley led the bevy of young beauties into Harding Howell & Co. Louisa had shopped here on many occasions before, but from the raptures that Penny and Ginny went into, it was clear that they had never seen such a profusion of lace, fans, gloves, and furs.

Penny, with her characteristic enthusiasm drew a pair of pink silk gloves onto her hands. "I must have these," she declared, "for my ball."

"I do think *white* gloves would be more the thing," said Mrs. Audeley, her brow puckered with consternation. But Penny would not be dissuaded. The silly girl wanted to stand out like a circus performer.

"Attracting notice is not always for the best," warned Louisa. It needed to be the right kind of notice. A lady strove to be classic. Elegant. Evocative. Penny might be pretty as a faerie princess, but vulgar taste would not serve her well in the ton.

"I *will* get these gloves," said Penny, ignoring the unsolicited advice.

Louisa shot the fractious Penelope a look of unadulterated disdain. "I should warn you, Miss Trafford, that you will never be considered an Incomparable with such outlandish taste."

"But at least I will also never be a governess." Penny's eyes sparkled with triumph as if she had pinked Miss Lymington with a fencing foil.

"I do not think you would qualify for the position," said Louisa acidly. The girl had no accomplishments, no education, no talent—except for clutching Gyles Audeley's arm whenever he entered the room.

"Girls," said Mrs. Audeley, using a voice of command that seemed incongruous coming from her kindly face. "We will not speak so to each other."

"Yes, Mrs. Audeley," said Penelope, but Louisa made no response. It stung, more than she liked to admit, to have her behaviour critiqued by Gyles' mother.

And yet, why should you care? The Audeleys mean nothing *to you.*

The Trafford sisters became distracted by all the scents in the perfumery section of the shop. Louisa's eyes narrowed as she saw Penny recklessly dabbing bergamot, vanilla, and musk on Milly's wrists. The girl would smell like a gentleman's club when her sister was done with her.

Mrs. Audeley, who had hung back beside Louisa, took the opportunity to commence a quiet tête-à-tête. "You are very young to be a governess."

"How old do you think I am?" said Louisa defensively.

"I should be surprised if you were more than one-and-twenty."

If only you were *one-and-twenty, then you would not be in this impossible situation!*

Louisa felt far more guilty lying to Mrs. Audeley than she had to Lord Kendall, so she kept silent on the subject and made no protestations about her advanced years.

"How did you gain the position teaching the Misses Trafford?"

"I answered an advertisement Lord Kendall had placed and took the post to Yorkshire."

"And yet, you do not seem to have been born a governess or even to be enthusiastic about the position. Had you no other options?"

"No, Mrs. Audeley." Louisa could see the soft sympathy in the older woman's face, but she had no wish to be pitied. She turned her shoulders to look the other way and end the conversation. Through an iron application of her will, she had not shed a single tear over her situation since bolting to Yorkshire. But if she were not careful now, Mrs. Audeley's kindly consideration would undo her. She would turn into a watering pot, and tears would draw all the attention that she needed so desperately to avoid.

Louisa felt Mrs. Audeley press her hand before moving on to gather up the strongly scented Trafford girls. She swallowed hard to subdue the rise of any further emotion before rejoining the group herself. Tears were a luxury she could not afford until she came into her inheritance.

CHAPTER EIGHTEEN

The Ball

GYLES HAD A STRONG premonition that tonight would be full of disappointment.

Penelope Trafford's long-awaited ball was finally coming to fruition. With Mrs. Audeley's careful planning, Lord Kendall had secured the most skilled musicians, the most festive decorations, and the most elegant guests that money could buy. His mother's efforts to launch their friend credibly into society would doubtless be a success. But Gyles was well-aware that the one person he wished to see would *not* be attending.

From the moment he had seen her standing apart from the rest in her dove-grey dress, Gyles knew that Miss Lymington was a flower that he must see bloom. She lingered in his memory, the Platonic form of ideal beauty that he had met in a garden, long ago. Except this Platonic form was very much flesh and blood—he had felt her body tremble beneath his hands when he reached out to steady her in the bookshop. He wished he could have held her longer and that Penny had not chosen that moment to interrupt.

There was a combination of qualities in Miss Lymington that he had never seen in another woman. She was statuesque, serious, incisive, intelligent, and sparkling as the rarest ruby in an undiscovered mine. If only he could convince her to hold more than thirty seconds' conference with him! But she was discreet as a damask rose, and regardless of how Gyles tried to draw her out, she kept her own counsel, thorns out and sepals furled.

He had no pretensions to his own position in society. He might be a gentleman, but he was of modest means. It would surprise no one should he marry a vicar's daughter, or a village wallflower, or a governess from Yorkshire. But Miss Lymington, despite her position in Lord Kendall's household, was none of these things. Even if she were not the missing Incomparable, Gyles was positive that Miss Lymington had not béen born to be a governess. She was someone who belonged in the courtyard of Carlton House, not someone who had climbed a wall to get there.

And yet, a walled garden was a very apt metaphor for Miss Lymington. Over the past few weeks, the governess' young charges had begged her to accompany them to the theatre or the other sights about town, but other than the one outing to Hatchard's, Miss Lymington was adamant that such was not her place. She would keep to the four walls of Kendall House, and she would not venture out into Grosvenor Square. Just yesterday, Gyles had overheard Ginny and Milly beg her to let them go downstairs tonight to watch a bit of the ball in their sister's honour, but Miss Lymington's edict stood firm—they would remain in the schoolroom and go to bed early.

Gyles arrived at the ball with his mother and received confirmation of his disappointment. Dark-haired Penelope and her uncle Lord Kendall beamed at them in the reception line, but there was no glimpse of the honey-coloured tresses that he most wished to see.

Viscount Landsdowne, the winner of the fencing match at Angelo's, led Penny out for the first dance, and Gyles found some nondescript creature to lead out onto the floor as well. Gyles danced the second set with Penny and then added his name to the last spare space on her dance card. He would do his duty to ensure that the debutante had her place in the sun even if the ballroom were as dull as a garden shovel for him.

The ball dragged on interminably. He danced with a few shy wallflowers and exchanged words with the handful of young bucks whom he had met in town. Mr. Tavinstock observed that Miss Trafford was fortunate that the Incomparable from last season had disappeared from the public eye, making Penelope, by far, the prettiest girl in the room. "Having never clapped eyes on last season's Incomparable," said Gyles, self-consciously, "I have no point of comparison."

"'Pon rep! She was a goddess," said another fellow whom Mr. Tavinstock introduced as Horatio Smythe. The tall, lanky fellow took a sip of his beverage. "Prime as punch. Made her an offer, but her uncle turned me down." He cocked his head and waved a long arm. "And so did she, come to think of it. But that was before I received my appointment from the Crown." He leaned in confidentially. "Diplomatic business. Adds an air of mystery. Ladies can't resist it."

"What's this, Smythe?" asked Tavinstock. "Are you part of our foreign service now? Going to Russia? France?"

"Confidential," said Mr. Smythe. He tapped his nose. "Sure I can trust you gentlemen to keep it quiet."

"Of course," said Gyles with a polite nod. He was not sure that it was in the Crown's best interest to entrust confidential information to Mr. Smythe if a little ballroom punch could loosen his tongue. "Mum's the word."

"The Crown's looking for a few more gentlemen eager to serve," said Mr. Smythe. His eyes came into sharper focus as he looked from Tavinstock to Gyles. "What about it, Gerrold?"

"Oh, not for me," demurred Tavinstock. "Not clever enough by half."

"Ha! Said as much myself," said Mr. Smythe, lapsing into inane laughter once again.

Deserting the bachelors' corner of the ballroom, Gyles looked around the room for the hundredth time, only to be met with another stab of disappointment. He walked past Solomon Digby, that lecherous old fellow he had seen at the park and at Angelo's. There was something rotten about that fellow, and it was not only his breath. He found it strange that Lord Kendall would invite the man, but then, Lord Kendall must be unaware that Miss Lymington could be the very lady Mr. Digby sought.

Eventually, overwhelmed by the swirling music, the incessant conversation, and the glow from the hundreds of candles in the ballroom, he stepped outside into the back courtyard to get a breath of air. Even in such a premier location as Grosvenor Square, the faint stench from the Thames assailed the nostrils. He missed the loamy smell of Derbyshire. He missed his garden of three hundred fifty-four rose bushes in forty-six different varieties.

Wandering over to the corner of the courtyard, he found the one rosebush that he brought to London with him, the

Sweet-Scented China Rose that had likely lost its chance to bloom this year for the first time. Reaching out, he stroked the soft sepals of a stunted bud. Could any flower thrive in soil so different from that in which it had been reared? Could a Derbyshire transplant truly bloom in the high society of London?

"Gyles," said a deep voice. Gyles turned back to see Lord Kendall framed by the lit door leading back into the house. "Your mother was feeling ill and went home with the Haverstalls. She asked me to tell you."

"Thank you," said Gyles, curious but not unduly alarmed. His mother had never been a robust woman, and she was sometimes laid low with headaches. He would have returned home too had he not one further duty still to be performed for Miss Trafford. "The ball is a great success, my lord," he said politely.

"I'm glad you think so," said Lord Kendall hoarsely. Gyles cocked his head and stared at him—there was a strained look about the earl's face that he did not remember ever seeing before, but it was not his place to ask questions.

They both returned to the ballroom, and Gyles counted down the minutes until the last dance began and he could fulfil his obligations to Miss Trafford.

"Wasn't this the most glorious evening?" asked Penelope, her little feet still floating like gossamer on the breeze even though the midnight hour had come and gone. Clearly, the exhaustion that had overtaken her elders was far from dulling her spirits.

"It was very fine." Gyles realised how insipid his words were the moment they came out, but Penelope was too in alt to notice. He pasted on a pleasant smile and tried to match her enthusiasm for the dance, but his thoughts kept wandering out of the ballroom and up the stairs. Was Miss Lymington listening wistfully to the strains of music below? Or had she fallen asleep in her attic room?

Following the last song, Lord Kendall seemed very keen to see the back of his guests. He shook hands and said farewells until only Gyles, Penelope, and an army of footmen were left. Gyles' mother had arranged for a bevy of temporary help to supplement the footmen who normally frequented the Kendall foyer, and they set to work clearing glasses, tidying tables, and putting away chairs.

Gyles walked out to the entryway and retrieved his hat. The evening was over, and he had never caught the barest glimpse of Miss Lymington. He knew he was behaving like a lovesick puppy, but he did not care. There were some women in the world worth making a cake of oneself—Helen of Troy, Cleopatra of Egypt, and Miss Lymington of London came readily to mind. Ah, well. He could visit the house tomorrow on the pretext of examining his rosebush, and perhaps he would be able to exchange a commonplace or two with the elusive governess.

"Uncle Bertie, Uncle Bertie!" cried two girlish voices, wafting down from the staircase. Gyles looked up at the ornate plasterwork ceiling and saw two pale faces surrounded by black curls peeking over the bannister.

"Girls," groaned Lord Kendall who had just come into the entrance hall. "It's late. Why have you not gone to bed?"

"We have something unpleasant to tell you," said the middle Trafford sister. "A fat man in a mauve waistcoat came upstairs into the family quarters where Miss Lymington was reading to us in the schoolroom."

By this time Penelope had danced her way down the corridor to stand beside Gyles in the entryway. "A man?" she gasped, clutching a hand to her heart.

"He was foxed," said the youngest sister, Milly.

Lord Kendall rushed up the stairs. "Are you all right? Did he harm you?"

"No," said Ginny, "he hardly noticed us. It was Miss Lymington who caught his attention."

"He called her a great many names," said Milly, "and chased her round and round the schoolroom table."

"Miss Lymington?" echoed Gyles in horror. He began to ascend the stairs with the speed of a Bond Street messenger boy, nearly bowling Lord Kendall over in his anxiety to reach the schoolroom.

CHAPTER NINETEEN

The Schoolroom

WHEN GYLES REACHED THE schoolroom, he discovered Solomon Digby bound to a chair and trussed like a fat pigeon while Miss Lymington stood guard, ruler in hand, in case the assailant should attempt to escape.

The girls explained that they had tripped him with a long length of curtain ribbon and bound him to the chair after he had been knocked unconscious. Gyles marvelled that the three of them had been able to lift the meaty blackguard into a sitting position.

Lord Kendall unfastened the makeshift gag and demanded to know why Mr. Digby had trespassed on his hospitality to assault his nieces and their governess.

"Governess!" Mr. Digby spat out, as if he had foul water in his mouth. "That's rich, Kendall. This girl here is none other than Louisa Lymington, the ward of the Duke of Warrenton."

Gyles looked at the governess to see if she would deny it, but her face merely settled into a marble mask.

"Indeed," said Lord Kendall coldly, confirming the identification. "What is that to you, Digby?"

Gyles blinked. He had known, deep in his bones, that Miss Lymington was the Incomparable. And it seemed that Lord Kendall had been aware of it as well.

Within minutes, the despicable Digby began blathering about how Lady Louisa had been promised to him by her guardian. "We're as good as engaged," he said with a squinty leer.

"I beg to differ," replied Miss Lymington. She raised the ruler. "I *never* agreed to marry you."

Gyles moved forward involuntarily and had to stop himself from interfering and standing between them. Of course she had not! Gyles could not conceive of a universe where a creature like Miss Lymington could be matched with a dog like Digby.

"Oh, come now," said the fat man in the mauve waistcoat. "You were sweet as cream to me the last time I saw you."

"That was to lull you into a false sense of security so that I could escape my uncle's house."

"Your uncle supported this man's suit?" demanded Gyles, his brow clouding even further. No wonder she was unused to kindness, to decency, to respect...to love.

"But why?" said Penelope, evidently of the same mind as Gyles on this matter. "Why would your uncle force you to marry this shocking excuse for a man?"

"Because my uncle is a greedy beast," said Miss Lymington, her tone clear and strong. "He inherited the dukedom two years ago when my father died, but the estate is bankrupt. My inheritance comes through my mother's side, and although I can't touch it until I come into my majority, neither can he. The only person who can is a husband. So, my uncle made a secret arrangement with Mr. Digby that if he allowed him to marry me, they would split my money once the marriage vows were said."

"But how did you become a governess?" asked Gyles. He had known that she was above his touch, but he could sense that the object of his affection was slipping even further out of reach now that her identity as a peeress was confirmed.

Miss Lymington—or as he should think of her now, Lady Louisa—explained how she had answered an advertisement for a governess in the wilds of Yorkshire and arrived to work for Lord Kendall. It would have suited her perfectly to have remained in Yorkshire, but when the Trafford sisters came to London for the season, she had been forced to travel with them. "And now that Digby has found me, he will go to my uncle Warrenton as soon as we release him. He will find me, and I shall be wholly in his power once again."

"Surely there is something we can do," said Gyles, racking his brain to think of some plan to protect Lady Louisa. He had saved her once from a cad at Carlton House, but a tangle of these proportions would require even greater ingenuity.

At this point, Miss Trafford proved her utter silliness by proposing the worst idea in the world since admitting a wooden horse into Troy. "I have it! Uncle Bertie must marry Miss Lymington!"

Gyles' eyes flew instantly to Lady Louisa's face. The scorn written across it was evident, soothing his worries that she would agree to Penelope's hare-brained scheme.

"But don't you see," continued Penelope, "it's just the thing! If Uncle Bertie married Miss Lymington, then Mr. Digby would be out of luck. And the Duke of Warrenton couldn't do a thing about it. How could anyone have any objection to that plan?"

"*I* object!" roared Mr. Digby.

Lady Louisa's fine eyebrows lifted. "I suppose Lord Kendall is *marginally* preferable. At least *he* doesn't wear shockingly hideous waistcoats, even though he is also old enough to be my father."

Gyles clenched his teeth.

"No. Absolutely not," said Lord Kendall, crossing his arms across his chest.

The three girls began to clutch at his elbows and plead with him until Lord Kendall shook them off in frustration. "I have no intention of marrying anyone other than Mrs. Audeley!"

"So that's the way the wind blows," said Gyles, locking eyes with him. Given his mother's constant presence at Kendall House—and the hint Mr. Heller had thrown his way at Angelo's—the thought of Lord Kendall as a stepfather should have occurred to him before now. But he had been too lost in his own concerns to see clearly. Now that he was considering it for the first time, he discovered that he rather liked the idea.

"Oh!" exclaimed Penelope, who was also fond of his mother. "If that's the case, then Miss Lymington had better find another gentleman to rescue her."

"I've done quite well rescuing myself so far," said Miss Lymington. Gyles looked at her with admiration. Yes, she had been incredibly resourceful. How many other young women would have had the wherewithal to run away to Yorkshire and hide from society as a governess? How many other young women would have kept their head about them when confronted by such a villain?

It was at this point that the restrained Mr. Digby began to be very unrestrained with his language. "You'll not hide from me again, you little baggage," he began. "I'll leave no stone in England unturned till your Uncle Warrenton makes good on his promise to me. And Kendall can make an honest woman of his own trollop—" That last comment ended before it had fully begun as Lord Kendall laid Mr. Digby out cold with a blow to the jaw.

At this display of violence, the girls' squeals began to rise to the rafters until Lord Kendall ordered them all to bed. "Lady Louisa, we'll speak in the morning," he said sternly. "And Gyles, could you send two footmen up on your way out? When Mr. Digby wakes up, I don't want him anywhere near this house."

Gyles nodded and left the schoolroom to do the earl's bidding. The butler and remaining footmen were all below-stairs by now, so he descended to the kitchen where they were tidying plates and scouring and counting the silver-ware. The temporary staff, who had only been hired for the night of the ball, had departed and left their liveries folded neatly on the kitchen worktable.

The butler expressed a modicum of surprise when informed that there was an unconscious man in the attic schoolroom who needed to be disposed of. He sent two of the remaining footmen upstairs to perform the unpleasant task and then added a third footman when Gyles informed him that the intruder was ponderously heavy.

His errand finished, Gyles looked about for Lord Kendall to inform him that Digby had been dealt with. The earl was not in his study, so Gyles went further down the hallway to the library. That room was also completely dark except for a few coals still smouldering in the fireplace. Gyles would have left immediately, but a peculiar sound caught his ears.

Thump—scrape. Thump—scrape.

It seemed to be coming from behind the wall. Seizing a candle from a sconce in the corridor, Gyles walked over to the wood panelling and saw a little door begin to open. And that was when he discovered Lady Louisa sliding her brass-bound travelling trunk down the servants' staircase as she tried to make good her escape from Kendall House.

CHAPTER TWENTY

The Trunk

LOUISA FLEXED HER SHOULDERS and gritted her teeth. This blasted trunk was as heavy as a sack of cannonballs, but there was no venal footman this time to carry it for her. Lord Kendall was well-loved in this house, and he would have been told in a trice if she'd asked one of his servants to perform any havey-cavey business.

She tripped over her cloak as she tried to manoeuvre the trunk down the narrow staircase, and her bulging reticule nearly slipped out of the pocket sewn into the side of her outer garment. She had no idea how she was going to get the trunk out into the courtyard and onto the street, but she had no intention of leaving with only the clothes on her back. She pushed open the small door leading out of the servants' staircase and shoved the mammoth portmanteau through it.

"My lady?" said a deep voice.

Her spine stiffened as she raised herself to her full height. She had been certain that the library would be unoccupied in the small hours of the morning, but instead, the faint light of the candle illuminated the lower half of a man's face, a man who knew that the woman tiptoeing out of the domestic staircase was no servant.

"Who are you?" she whispered fiercely, already suspecting the truth as she asked the question.

He lifted the candle to show his face more fully, revealing tanned features with a firm chin and soulful brown eyes. His wavy chestnut hair was more untamed than usual, and his cravat had wilted over his black evening wear. But his black coat had not crumpled a bit, filled out with the strong shoulders that she had first noticed in Hatchard's book shop. Shoulders attached to arms, arms attached to hands, hands that—in a brighter world—ought to be encircling her waist.

Louisa's face flamed red in the darkness. In that moment, she knew that if Gyles Audeley wanted to stop her flight from Kendall House, he could. He had only to lift a finger and she would be halted. He had only to speak a word and she would be frozen in place. And in that moment, she hated him for the power that he had over her.

He stepped forward gently as if she were a deer in the forest thicket that he did not want to startle. "Might I assist you?"

Louisa's insides began to churn.

Silly, silly girl. You know hardly anything of this man other than a girlish memory your imagination has expanded to herculean proportions. He is only offering help because of his good breeding—it is the same milksop politeness he displays to Penelope Trafford.

The annoyance provoked by imagining Miss Trafford wilting on Gyles Audeley's arm lent an edge of exasperation to her voice. "Yes, I could use your assistance. This trunk is too heavy for me to lift without dragging it, and I need it carried out through the courtyard to the corner of the street."

The long clock in the library chimed three o'clock. "A strange time of night to be toting a trunk," observed Gyles. His voice was still soft. Soothing. Gentle.

"Lord Kendall asked me to leave the premises immediately."

Liar! Why would you tell him that? He'll think the less of you for it later.

"But where will you go?"

"That is none of your affair," she blurted out, before she remembered that she needed a little more honey to catch the fly that would carry her brass-bound trunk. "Please, Mr. Audeley, if you would be so kind."

He looked at her thoughtfully, the candle casting a warm light on his tan face. "Very well, my lady. If you will wait in the courtyard, I will follow with your trunk."

There was an earnestness about Gyles' face that made Louisa believe him. Through the vagaries of fate, this eccentric gardener with his thoughtful consideration might be her godsend once again.

She nodded her agreement and, clutching the reticule that she had laid atop the trunk, made her way through the dark library and out the short corridor that led to the back door. The house was all quiet and the door was locked, but she had kept her wits about her the last few weeks and had pocketed the butler's spare key when no one was looking. After a few seconds fumbling at the lock, she opened the door and slipped outside. The cold night air slithered inside her cloak, but her pounding heart kept her warm enough for what lay ahead.

She closed the door behind her and began to wait on her accomplice. Two minutes passed. Then five. Either the trunk was too heavy for Gyles Audeley, or he had decided to betray her flight and was even now shaking Lord Kendall awake from his bed. Her violet-brown eyes sparked with annoyance. Should she count the trunk—and the clothes that proclaimed her status as a lady—as a loss and move on? Or should she go back and see what was taking him so long?

They'll put the hounds on your trail before long. You can't count on Lord Kendall to keep you safe. And your uncle and Mr. Digby will be at the door as soon as morning light dawns with that special licence up their sleeves.

After another five minutes, she decided she no longer had the luxury of waiting. She was just moving toward the courtyard gate when the back door opened and Mr. Audeley stepped outside. By the light of a distant streetlamp, she could make out the large trunk perched on his left shoulder. His right hand was clutching some kind of bag or satchel, and he leaned awkwardly to the side as he balanced his heavy load.

"This way," she hissed, forging ahead toward the street. Gyles followed her, stopping for a few seconds in front of a planter box in the courtyard. She rolled her eyes. Was Gyles Audeley so captivated by his prize rose bush that he could not resist looking in on it in the middle of the night? Would he need to stop and count the number of buds and leaves on each branch?

With relief, Louisa discovered that the courtyard gate was well oiled. There was no grinding squeak of iron hinges as she pushed it open. She remembered the last time she had walked the London streets in the dead of night, only to see Mr. Smythe tumble from a hackney. Would there be any drivers passing Kendall House at this hour? Or had they all taken their custom elsewhere now that the ball-goers had dispersed?

The clatter of wheel rims on cobblestones sent a wave of relief through her. "Cabby!" said a deep voice, and she was surprised to discover that Mr. Audeley had hailed the man without waiting for her to do so.

The hackney came to a stop and Louisa began to give the driver instructions while Gyles fastened the trunk to the back of the vehicle. She climbed inside only to have the door open a moment later and another figure take the seat opposite her.

"What are you doing?" she demanded, recognizing the interloper's face by the light of the carriage lantern.

"I'm coming with you," Gyles Audeley announced, tossing his satchel onto the seat next to him. But even though his tone was pleasant, there was a mulish set to his chin and his brown eyes glinted with determination. Instinctively, Louisa Lymington knew that this pursuer would be far harder to elude than those she had fled in the past.

CHAPTER TWENTY-ONE
Pawn Shop

A S THE WHEELS BEGAN to rattle through the streets, Louisa heard the echo of another set of carriage wheels on the road behind them. "What is that?" she asked, senses heightened by the magnitude of the threats that faced her. "Is someone following us?"

Why did you think you could trust him? No doubt he alerted Lord Kendall of your flight, and now a whole troop of footmen are following to bring you back.

Gyles leaned back on the seat placidly. "It's my coachman. I sent him north as a decoy."

"A decoy?"

"Well, yes. I assume our destination is not Scotland?"

"Certainly not!" Louisa would be as likely to leg shackle herself to the hackney driver as she would to...anyone else. The whole point of her flight was to elude marriage until her fortune and her future should be entirely under her own control. She would not be visiting any anvil parson in Scotland, and she would be shedding Gyles Audeley's company as soon as possible.

"I've sent my carriage north so that others will assume it is. Perhaps your uncle will take the bait and follow."

It was a clever ploy, and possibly useful. And yet, Louisa could not like the way this absent-minded gardener was taking mastery of the situation. "How presumptuous of you, sir!"

"I beg your pardon, my lady," said Gyles, without taking affront. "I daresay presumption has always been a failing of mine." Louisa narrowed her eyes, but in the dark carriage it was impossible to see whether he was laughing at her.

It's true. Only a presumptuous young man would climb a prince's garden wall. Only a presumptuous young man would take cuttings of rose bushes without being invited.

And yet, Louisa could not dislike him for it. There was something eminently satisfying about a man who knew what he wanted and took a chance to obtain it.

The hackney turned at the corner and headed southeast through London. The sounds of the other carriage swiftly disappeared, superseded by the faint chirping of town birds as the black night gave way to the grey of morning. They were passing under the shadow of St. Paul's now, and Louisa was alternately relieved and disconcerted that her travelling partner kept silent throughout the trip.

What is Gyles Audeley mulling over? What sinister motive does he have for following you?

When she could stand it no longer, she blurted out a question. "What are you thinking about?"

He smiled sheepishly as if startled from a reverie. "The variety of pollinators in the country as opposed to pollinators in the town. The chirping birds put it into my head."

Louisa was taken aback. "What an odd matter to fix your mind upon."

"Yes, well, I suppose most gentlemen would rather talk of horses, or cards, or brandy. What are *you* thinking about?" Gyles leaned forward, elbows on knees, still surprisingly handsome in his evening wear.

No one has ever asked you that question before.

"Money," said Louisa, looking away from him and out the window into the grey light. "And how to get it quickly to pay for travelling expenses.

Gyles shook his head. "You took me completely unprepared tonight, my lady. I'm afraid I have little to nothing in my purse. If this hackney takes us much farther, it will be more than I can pay him."

"I've instructed him to take us to a pawn shop in Cheapside." Louisa opened her reticule that she had kept hidden in her cloak and took out a string of black jet beads. "It's a good place to trade a few pieces of jewellery for coin."

"I hope you are not thinking of parting with family heirlooms to finance your flight?" He seemed alarmed by the idea as if a necklace or a bracelet could mean something more to someone than a set of sparkling stones on a string.

"I am not a creature of sentiment, Mr. Audeley." Louisa patted the heavy reticule. "I took possession of all my mother's jewellery before my uncle could use it to pay for his spendthrift style of life. He might control my pin money, but at least I can convert gemstones to ready cash. It's how I paid for my trip to Yorkshire."

And it's how you'll pay for your new life in Paris. But better to tell Gyles Audeley nothing of that. You must get rid of him before you set out for Plymouth.

The hackney rolled to a stop in front of a shop with three golden balls suspended above the door. Gyles cleared his throat. "If you would like me to negotiate for you, sometimes a gentleman's presence is helpful in...these parts of London."

"Are you conversant, then, with the customs of pawnbrokers, Mr. Audeley?"

"Not particularly," he admitted.

"I thought not. You may follow me inside." Louisa would do the negotiating herself, but it would be helpful for the owner to catch a glimpse of Gyles Audeley's broad shoulders. It was a sad truth with which she was well familiar, that a lady unprotected was a lady that many sought to take advantage of. She would use Mr. Audeley's masculine services one last time and then send him on some fool's errand while she slipped away on her own.

CHAPTER TWENTY-TWO

Livery

GYLES HELD TIGHTLY TO his satchel and watched Louisa negotiate with the pawnbroker. Zounds, but she was magnificent to behold! He could not imagine any other woman of his acquaintance sweeping into such a grimy establishment before dawn had broken, quelling the proprietor's questions with a word, and demanding that he give her a fair price for the gems she was offering.

"Hermes' wig and wing feathers," muttered the fellow, clearly ready for bed after a night of unsavoury business with pickpockets and cutpurses. His thin grey hair lay combed across his balding head like the strings of a greasy harp. He pinched the jet beads between finger and thumb and held them up to the light of a lantern. "These're worth a pair of guineas, they are. But I'm feelin' generous, so let's say three."

"Let us say thirty," said Louisa confidently. The jet beads were doubtless worth triple that amount, but Gyles could see she knew quite well how much silver could be wrung from a skinflint. In the end, the fellow offered her twenty guineas for the string of jet and then surprised everyone—including himself—by giving her another forty guineas for the sapphire brooch she placed on his counter.

"An' will you be comin' back to redeem them?" demanded the pawnbroker.

"No," said Louisa. "I'll not be returning to London anytime soon."

Gyles looked at her curiously. Where did she plan to run to this time? There was no newspaper advertisement to answer. There was no governess position to take.

He listened closely as the hackney driver asked for their next destination. Louisa gave the address for a nearby coaching inn in Cheapside. Apparently, she had thought through this venture thoroughly and was as familiar with this part of London as Gyles was with the market towns in Derbyshire.

Within minutes, they had arrived at a bustling innyard bearing a sign with a two-headed swan. Louisa paid the driver and then handed Gyles a guinea. "Mr. Audeley, might I trouble you to secure us some breakfast?"

"Of course, my lady," said Gyles, realising as she said the word that he was hungry indeed. Staying up all night tended to do that to a man. So did running away from home on the heels of an unpredictable heiress.

Gyles saw the porter from the inn unload Louisa's portmanteau and drop it in a shaded corner of the courtyard. Louisa, still wearing her voluminous cloak, crossed over and sat on the trunk. The place looked well-lit and safe enough to leave a resourceful woman. Gyles ducked his head under the swinging sign of the double-necked swan and went up to the counter.

"Might I have two cups of ale and two plates of whatever is hot—"

"Wait your turn there!" bellowed a big fellow covered with a layer of dust and grime over what must have once been a proper suit of clothes.

The innkeeper's wife bobbed Gyles an apologetic curtsy. "Beggin' your pardon, sir, but I'll serve the drivers first if I may. They canna be late and must keep to their schedule. Won't be more'n a minute afore I can put together some victuals for you."

"Of course," said Gyles, never one to insist on his own consequence. He crossed his arms and leaned against the wall, an incongruous figure in his fancy eveningwear amongst an unwashed room of drivers, drovers, and harbour men.

Ten minutes later, the grimy giant took his plate of hot food from the counter and smirked at Gyles as he brushed by him. "That's the last of it," he said with a snide laugh.

"Never fear. I'll warm some more porridge," said the round innkeeper's wife, tucking a few frazzled curls back into her cap. "Won't take more'n a minute or two."

Gyles had a fairly good idea of how long a "minute" might take at the Swan with Two Necks. He decided to make use of the time. "Might there be a private room I can step inside while I'm waiting?"

"Oh, indeed there is, sir," said the woman. She gestured to the open door that led off the main dining area. Gyles, shouldering his satchel, stepped between the men drinking at the tables and went into the adjoining room. It was a private parlour with a fireplace, a table, and two chairs—modest, clean, and perfect for what Gyles needed to do next.

Gyles shut the door and drew the curtains on the narrow windows. Then, finally opening his satchel, he removed a suit of green and grey livery along with a set of silver-buckled shoes and a curled horsehair wig. He had seized it from the kitchen table before bringing Lady Louisa's trunk out the back door of Kendall House, leftover livery from the hired footmen who had helped at Penelope's ball. The footmen Mrs. Audeley had hired were tall and well-formed, and the uniform fit Gyles well. The shoes were a little tight, but he supposed he could manage the discomfort for a while.

Gyles had never worn a wig, but choking down his distaste for something so foreign, he placed it over his untamed chestnut hair. A quick glance at the distorted reflection of himself in a polished pewter sconce showed that it was not askew. He packed the evening wear back into the satchel, just in case he might need it again sometime in the future.

There. Now he was ready to pursue Lady Louisa with propriety. An unmarried gentleman travelling with a lady would compromise her reputation. But a footman was *de rigeur* for a woman of her station. Still, it would look a little odd that she did not have her own carriage—he would have to remedy that at some point.

The porridge the innkeeper's wife had promised was still not ready, so Gyles strode outside to check on his charge. Ducking under the sign with the double-necked swan, he looked around in the early morning light and frowned. The heavy portmanteau he had expected to see in the corner of the courtyard was missing. The cloaked figure had disappeared as well.

Where could she have gone?

The large, dirty fellow whom Gyles had had the misfortune to cross at the counter was leaning against the post of the porch, quaffing his breakfast ale. "Ho there," said Gyles crisply. "Where's the lady that was sitting here on a leather trunk?"

"That fancy-piece?" The big man nodded toward a black and red carriage that was wheeling out of the courtyard and toward the road. "She took the coach to Plymouth."

Without a word, Gyles began to run. The unfamiliar, silver-buckled shoes pinched with each step, but nevertheless, he increased his pace with each stride. With one hand he held onto his satchel. With the other he held onto his wig.

"Cor!" said the fellow, calling after him. "Ain't you the gentleman that tried to snatch my place in line?"

Gyles had no time to answer. His silver-buckled shoes pounded the ground as he passed the guard at the back of the coach. He came level with the front of the coach, just as the driver was slowing down to make the turn onto the main road.

"Oi, what's this all about?" the driver demanded as Gyles yanked his precarious wig down over his forehead and pulled himself up into the seat beside him.

"Nearly lost my position waiting on the porridge," said Gyles, affecting a rougher accent than was his wont. He jerked a thumb to the body of the carriage behind them. "My mistress is inside."

"Oh, that one?" said the driver. Clearly, he was aware which of his passengers was quality enough to employ a footman.

"Care if I sit up here with you?" asked Gyles.

"Hmph," said the driver complainingly. "Should've been here five minutes ago so's I didn't have to stow her luggage. Trunk's as heavy as Prince George's coffin'll be."

Gyles rubbed an aching shoulder sympathetically. "Don't I know it."

The driver clucked. "Well, at least you'll be the one unloading it when we stop."

Gyles gave a grim smile and set his wig firmly in place. He might regret his actions later, but he was not about to let Lady Louisa depart in an unknown mail coach without some sort of protection. She would not thank him for it—of that, he was certain—but he would not be able to live with himself if he did not intervene. Even if it meant an abandoned rosebush, an itchy head, a ridiculously old-fashioned coat and pantaloons, and silver-buckled shoes that hurt like the blazes.

CHAPTER TWENTY-THREE

Pebble

LOUISA FELT HER APLOMB start to wilt as the carriage ride dragged on interminably. The driver stopped every hour or so to change the horses. Since she had no need to use the necessary, she elected to stay inside in her seat where she would draw the least attention.

Fortunately, none of the other passengers were overly curious about the silent young lady in the voluminous cloak. A large, heavily scented shop wife tried to offer her a stale bun, but Louisa refused it even though her stomach was growling.

Best not to take anything anyone offers. You can take care of yourself, and you would not wish to encourage further acquaintance.

Louisa remembered the breakfast she had sent Gyles Audeley to fetch for her at the Swan with Two Necks. A wistful feeling—no doubt, hunger pangs—began to afflict her insides.

Of course, you could have eaten breakfast if you had not bolted for the mail coach in Cheapside. But then you would still be saddled with Gyles Audeley, so going hungry is all for the best.

Louisa swallowed. She had sneered at the idea of Scotland as a destination, but would staying with Gyles Audeley really have been so bad? She did not want to escape her uncle's clutches just to turn over her person and fortune to the first man who was kind to her. But out of all the men she knew, had she ever met anyone better than that eccentric gardener from Derbyshire?

Stupid girl. A man who considers the number and variety of town and country pollinators while riding in a carriage with a beautiful woman? You cannot be serious.

And yet, despite his strange preoccupation with cultivating rose bushes, he *had* managed to put that aside and be there for her exactly when she had needed him. At Carlton House in the stone pavilion. At Kendall House with her too-heavy trunk. It was pleasant having someone there who cared about her interests. Someone who took the time to assist her into an armchair when she felt faint. Someone who had the sense to deploy a decoy carriage when she needed secrecy.

Fiddlesticks! You're used to taking care of yourself. You do it better than anyone else ever has. Gyles Audeley just happened to be there at the right moment, and he would have done the same for anyone. He's a Good Samaritan, not a hero.

Finally, at midday, when the carriage stopped at a little town east of Guildford, Louisa resolved to rouse the frozen blood in her limbs and find some nourishment. She waited for the large lady with the basket of stale buns to step out into the innyard and then followed her out the carriage door.

"Milady," said a footman in green and silver, inclining his head as he handed her down the steps and out the carriage. She took his hand without thought and then advanced towards the small inn with its stained brickwork and broken shutters.

How peculiar that this out-of-the-way inn should have a footman in livery...livery that looked striking like the Kendall House uniform. Louisa paused, turned around, and gasped. The fellow in the green coat with the silver frog fastenings was none other than Gyles Audeley.

Conscious that they might be observed, Louisa nodded her head towards the little garden patch by the side of the inn. Gyles, understanding her unspoken message, followed her to that secluded spot.

"What on earth are you doing here?"

"Keeping you company in your travels, my lady."

"I don't *need* your company."

He said nothing to that. Clearly, he did not believe her.

"And I don't want it either."

"Apologies, my lady, but I can't let you travel alone. It wouldn't be honourable of me." His face was all earnestness, and if Louisa did not know better, she would have said he was speaking the truth.

But how could a man be that quixotic? He must *have some ulterior motive for following you. Deep down, he's no different from your father, from your uncle, or from Mr. Digby.*

"I suppose you think this a clever plan on your part—to wait until we're far from home and then force me into marriage with you so you'll have control of my fortune."

He let out a long-suffering sigh that made her own objection feel childish. "That has never been my intention."

"I don't see what other possible intention you could have."

"Don't you?"

She was a tall woman, but she still had to look upwards to meet his brown eyes. The pressure of his gaze was too much. She dropped her stare and focused instead on the left shoulder of his green livery.

"Upon my word, sir, you are a *pebble* in my shoe."

"One could be worse things," said her pursuer with a dismissive wave of the hand. "Now for my question: will you run away again if I try to secure you some breakfast?"

Louisa's treacherous stomach chose that moment to grumble. "I...suppose not."

"Good," said Gyles briskly. "The driver says we'll stop at this inn for half an hour, so with your permission, I'll secure a private parlour for your use."

Louisa stared at him and said nothing.

He turned to leave the vegetable garden and went inside the inn. Louisa noted that he was limping a little in his footman's shoes. Brow furrowed, she followed at a slower pace, and by the time she caught sight of the innkeeper, she discovered a private parlour with a fire and respectable nuncheon waiting for her.

CHAPTER TWENTY-FOUR

Plymouth

I T WAS NOT LONG before Gyles came to discover why Louisa's leather-bound trunk was so heavy. They spent the night in Southampton, and he obtained a room for her from the innkeeper and a bunk in the stables for himself. When he knocked on her door to ask if she needed anything, Louisa was standing by a chair that held a dozen gowns she had unearthed from the trunk. They were much finer dresses than she had worn as a governess. He had never suspected so many gowns could fit in one trunk. Dropping a navy-coloured gown in Gyles' arms, Louisa ordered him to find a maid to put it in a clothes press and rid it of its wrinkles.

"Yes, milady," said Gyles patiently. He could tell that Louisa was punishing him with her hauteur. Punishing him for pursuing her against her will. But how could he abandon her now? Despite her poise and high-handed manner, she was still a young lady alone in a world filled with rum coves and ruffians.

The following morning, Louisa emerged from her room in the elegant navy carriage dress and a smart capote bonnet. She looked every inch the daughter of a duke, and Gyles could see the innkeeper and the denizens of Southampton touch their forelocks a little more readily and make a leg a little deeper. The governess was gone completely. She looked far too fine a lady to ride the mail coach to Plymouth.

Gyles was not surprised when she bade him find a livery stable and hire a private post chaise to take her the rest of the way to Plymouth. He had never done such a thing before, but taking the guineas Lady Louisa entrusted to him, he inquired of the innkeeper where a carriage and driver might be procured. Before half an hour had passed, he arrived back at the inn, sitting inside a smart equipage that would not embarrass the daughter of a duke.

Given her behaviour last night, he expected no thanks from Louisa. His expectations were met to perfection. "You'll not be riding inside with me," she announced brusquely and ordered him to secure the trunk to the back of the carriage.

As a governess, her words had been cool and uninviting, but ever since he had donned a footman's garb, she had put up an even sharper palisade of defence. It was the sort of bristling resistance a wild animal might put up when backed into a corner.

"Yes, milady," said Gyles, touching his forelock as he had often seen servants do. He took a deep breath and climbed up beside the driver he had just hired for the trip. He had waited years for a rosebush to bloom. He could afford to endure thorns a little while longer.

The third day of travel brought them to Plymouth. Gyles had wondered at this destination, but it was not long before he discovered that Plymouth was just a stopping spot along the journey.

As he untied the trunk from the carriage, she gave him a curt nod. "You'd best go back to Southampton with the driver and make your way to London from there."

"Why?" asked Gyles. "Are you answering a governess advertisement in Plymouth?"

Her pretty, full lips quirked up in a mischievous smile at that. "No, Mr. Audeley. I'm taking ship to France."

"France!" He thought that nothing she did could surprise him anymore, but this daring cast of the die upset all his notions of what she was capable. "But...Bonaparte. The war! How can you even achieve it?"

"Merchant and diplomatic vessels are still allowed through the blockade in small numbers. I'll cross from Plymouth to Morlaix with no trouble."

"Have you ever been to France?"

"No," she admitted. "But it is my mother's country, and I speak French like a native."

To Gyles, her ability to speak fluent French seemed little guarantee of safety. "Do you have papers? Do you have relatives who will take you in?"

She did not answer those questions. Gyles could only suppose that the answer was no.

"I'm not afraid, Mr. Audeley. It's the one place my uncle will never find me. I have enough jewels to live off, and English women are a rarity there—I daresay I shall make quite the impression."

Gyles did not doubt it. With her honey-gold hair, creamy white skin, and voluptuous figure, she was the epitome of an English shepherdess. And English shepherdesses should not go alone into a pack of French wolves. "Let me help you find a ship," he said, seeking to buy more time as he considered what to do. At least he could make sure she was not taken advantage of by some unscrupulous sailing captain.

"Very well," said Louisa with a shrug, as if she did not care whether he went or stayed.

And so began their quest along the docks of Plymouth, the brine of the salt air a strange taste on their lips after the smell of loamy dirt along the road. Plymouth wharf bustled with sailors and marines. Several ships were under repair in the town's drydocks, and the calls of carpenters mingled with the sound of hammers driving bolts into beams and keels. Dozens of the ships in port were seaworthy, but after a long afternoon of queries, the tired travellers discovered that only a handful of them were willing to cross over to Morlaix. None of them were taking additional passengers.

At the last ship, Louisa demonstrated just how much steel lay behind those velvety eyes and heart-shaped face. "What do you mean there are no cabins available?" she demanded of the officer on the wharf. Somehow, the scorn stamped on her face did nothing to diminish her beauty.

The officer shrugged. "You have no booking. We are full."

"You can make room."

The harried officer rubbed his dark sideburns with irritation. "I am not God, my lady. I cannot make the ship larger at will."

Gyles, standing back four or five paces with the trunk on his shoulder and satchel dangling from his other arm, shifted from one foot to the other to alleviate the discomfort of his tight-fitting shoes. His head itched, and he balanced the trunk with one hand to rub his right temple—but then remembered just in time that his wig was liable to shift positions if he scratched it too vigorously.

"No, but perhaps you can make the ship smaller, too small for someone who already has a booking." Louisa reached into her reticule and pulled out a handful of guineas.

The officer blinked and hesitated, but after a moment, he reached out his hand to pocket the coin. "Very well, mistress, there is one passenger cabin that is not filled yet—for a wine merchant and his wife. I will tell them when they come that there is no more room." He looked around nervously to make sure his conduct was not being observed by any of his fellow shipmates. "What name shall I add to the manifest?"

"The Comtesse Dammartin," said Louisa, pronouncing the name in flawless French.

Gyles stared at her with curiosity. Was this yet another new identity? She said it so easily as if the name were long familiar to her tongue.

"Do you have a maid with you?" asked the officer, still suspicious. It was highly irregular for a "lady" to embark on a voyage without another female in her entourage.

"No," she said, her eyes raking him over as if he were stupid.

"A lady cannot travel alone." The man was adamant. It was clear that not even another handful of guineas would sway him.

Gyles took a few steps forward and looked her in the eye. He was willing. He would go.

Louisa pursed her lips as if trying to make up her mind between two evils. "My English maid wishes to remain here with her family, and my French maid will meet us at Morlaix. But my footman will come aboard and tend to my belongings. That will satisfy your requirement, yes, that I do not travel alone? I assume you have room for him below decks?"

The officer began to grumble again about his lack of space and lack of divine powers to create more, but another guinea from the lady caused him to admit that he could locate a spare hammock.

"And what is the name I should put on the manifest?"

Louisa looked back at Gyles, standing stoically in his green knee breeches and grey stockings. She gave a mischievous smile.

"You may write down Pebble. Gyles Pebble."

CHAPTER TWENTY-FIVE

Morlaix

MORLAIX, FRANCE ~ NOVEMBER 1810

THE CHANNEL CROSSING PASSED without incident. Louisa retired to her cabin away from the stares of the sailors and the whispers of the other passengers. She elected to remain in her carriage dress all night since she could not borrow a maid to loosen her stays as she had at the roadside inns. Gyles had come to her door twice, once to bring her food and once to ask if she needed anything, but that was hardly an office she could ask him to perform. Louisa's cheeks reddened simply remembering the firm pressure of his hand on her waist at Hatchard's.

You're glad he came with you, aren't you? Well, you won't be when it comes time to discard him in Paris. And then what? He'll return to England and inform Uncle Nigel of your whereabouts. Your only hope then is that Uncle Nigel is too cucumberish to come after you. Although, Mr. Digby certainly has the blunt to finance a foxhunt.

When it came time to disembark at Morlaix, Louisa waited impatiently for Gyles to collect her trunk from the cabin. "*Zut alors!* You smell like a tavern," she said, sniffing loudly as Gyles ducked his head to enter the cabin through the low door frame.

He gave a lopsided grin. "Our crew is quite fond of rum. It's a miracle the steersman took us into the harbour without mishap."

"And are *you* fond of rum, Mr. Audeley?"

"Certainly not," he said with mock gravity. "I wouldn't wish to lose my position due to overindulgence."

"Hmm. I doubt your employer could get rid of you even if she tried. Did you enjoy your time below decks?"

"Indeed. Although I had some ado to convince the sailors that my mistress was not a French spy."

"A spy!" Louisa had never considered that anyone would cast her in such a role. "How did you convince them?"

Again, Gyles grinned. "Why, I told them you were an English one."

Louisa did not know whether to believe him or to rebuke him for teasing her, so she dropped the subject entirely.

They disembarked from the ship and were detained at the wharf by a customs agent eager to see their papers. "*Je suis la Comtesse Dammartin,*" said Louisa confidently. Inside, she said a silent prayer that the customs agent would not harbour the same suspicions as the sailors had. "My husband has my papers, but he is not here yet."

The customs agent's beady eyes became even beadier. "Your husband, *madame*? *Le Comte* is coming here?"

"*Mais oui*. Surely, you do not expect a beautiful woman to tend to something so tedious as passports? I am the Countess Dammartin. I have been visiting England, and I am now very tired of the food and the fashion. *Sacrebleu*, these Englishmen eat like animals and dress like barbarians. I wish to go home to my chateau outside Paris." She looked at him imperiously, and somehow, miraculously, her bravado worked.

"See that you obtain the proper papers when you get to Paris," said the customs agent admonishingly, but he allowed Louisa and Gyles to pass through the line, his awe of the imaginary count enough to overcome his love of bureaucracy.

"How did you manage that?" asked Gyles quietly. Louisa realised that he had understood none of her French conversation. He was walking by her side in the street, carefully guiding them around the refuse of discarded rope and broken glass that littered the area.

"Simple. One has only to abuse the English, and the French will be on your side." She smiled as a memory came to mind. "My mother used to complain dreadfully about the English cooking and the lack of proper textiles or skilful seamstresses. She was positively scathing when she wanted to be...and she *always* got her way."

Gyles took her elbow and stopped her from stepping out into the street as a one-horse cabriolet flew past.

"A strong woman, your mother."

"She had to be, or she would not have escaped the Terror. She knew what was coming and left for England before they stormed the Bastille." Louisa watched his fingers slide free from her elbow. They stepped into the street towards a livery stable and the growing aroma of horses and manure. "Although, as far as mothers go," she said shyly, "I think I prefer yours."

It was true. There was a warmth and kindness about Mrs. Audeley that the Comtesse Dammartin had entirely lacked.

"I have a great partiality for her as well."

"She must be terribly worried about you," said Louisa, her words falling over each other as she lost her usual sense of poise. "You ought to take the next passage back. I'll pay your fare. You would not want her to suffer."

"I daresay Lord Kendall will see her through it," said Gyles, falling a step behind her as was more proper for a footman. "And if I took passage now, *I* should be terribly worried about leaving an unprotected lady behind."

"Always the *preux chevalier*," said Louisa, regaining the sarcastic edge to her voice. "I would think you would have discovered by now that I am able to take care of myself."

"*Mais oui*," replied Gyles in the worst approximation of a French accent that Louisa had ever heard. He touched his forelock with his free hand in the semblance of respect. "Milady always knows best."

Louisa could not tell whether he was agreeing with her or rebuking her.

CHAPTER TWENTY-SIX

On the Road

ONCE AGAIN, GYLES WAS forced to prove his usefulness by finding a carriage for hire. The task was more difficult this time since the French language was a closed book to him. He followed his nose to a livery stable, and after pleading his case in English before a group of haughty French coachmen, finally found one who would take pity on him.

A mountain of a man rose from his seat on a barrel—bearded, stern, and smelling of horses, onions, and pipe tobacco. "Paris?"

Gyles nodded.

The man grunted and beckoned for Gyles to follow him. He brought him to the other side of the stable where an old but serviceable coach stood waiting. He gave Gyles a searching look.

Guessing rightly, Gyles dug into his pocket and drew out the remainder of the money Louisa had given to him.

The man shook his head at the British pounds. "*Non. Francs.* You will pay me *en Paris.*" Taking out a pipe and tobacco from a pouch, he lit it and let out a puff of smoke that swallowed Gyles whole like fog on the Thames.

Thus began their journey from the coast to the capital. Gyles sat up on the box with the driver and learned through mono-syllables and gesticulation that the man's name was Jacques Martin. Their conversation could not go much further than that, and finding Jacques' cloud of tobacco more pungent than was desirable, Gyles spent most of his time with head turned away, observing the countryside.

Despite the French penchant for claiming superiority over everything English, the condition of the French roads was far worse than anything Gyles had ever encountered. These thor-oughfares had not been tended to since Marie Antoinette lost her head, and probably not for decades prior. The trees and undergrowth often encroached on the road itself, leaving all sorts of low-hanging branches and leafy copses where danger could be concealed.

On the afternoon of the second day, Gyles was hoping to see new varieties of hedge roses, but instead he saw two horsemen ride out from the trees and make straight for them. Both men had dirty muslin scarves tied over their faces and pistols in one hand. Upon spotting them, Jacques immediately put down his pipe and began to whip up the horses as if the Furies themselves were riding behind.

"What's going on?" demanded Gyles.

"*Les brigands!*" Jacques fumbled with one hand in the oil-cloth bag behind the seat. He kept his other hand on the swing-ing reins. Pulling out a flintlock pistol, he thrust it in Gyles' hands and then unearthed another one for himself. Apparently, the man had driven through this countryside enough times to come prepared.

"Er, do you really mean for me to shoot them?" asked Gyles, seeing that the pistol was primed and loaded.

Even if he had understood the question, Jacques was too busy urging his team on to answer. The two riders were close to the carriage now. The pounding hoofbeats of their horses diverged as each moved towards one side of the fast-paced coach. Gyles turned around in his seat. The fellow on his side had almost come parallel to the carriage window.

He hesitated. The gun felt foreign in his hand. He had a theoretical knowledge of how pistols worked, and he had even fired them once or twice. But his father had not been fond of hunting, and he had no brothers, cousins, or friends enamoured with shooting. There had never been occasion to become proficient with a flintlock.

The gigantic driver gripped the reins in his teeth and, wheeling about in the seat, sent a shot behind him, straight into the shoulder of the approaching highway marauder. The man let out a cry of pain, and his horse slowed and veered off the road again.

Gyles swallowed. Clearly, it was his responsibility to take down the man on the right side of the carriage. He levelled the pistol at the man's galloping figure and then jerked it upwards again. What if he missed and the man pried open Louisa's carriage door? What if he didn't miss and shot the man straight through the heart?

As the latter did not impinge on Louisa's safety, it seemed the lesser of two evils. He had just made up his mind to take the shot when a report rang out behind him. At first, he thought the highwayman must have fired, but craning his neck around, he saw that the second rider was slowing to a halt, reins slack, hands pressed against his thigh on which a dark spot was spreading.

Jacques continued driving at a brisk pace until they arrived at the next village. Then, screeching to a stop in front of the churchyard, he nodded at his companion.

Gyles leapt down from the seat with the speed of a greyhound and opened the carriage door. There was Louisa in her stylish carriage dress and bonnet, a short-barrelled pistol resting beside her on the bench. She was not in hysterics, as Penelope would have been, but Gyles was surprised to see her heart-shaped face so calm after such an ordeal.

"Was it you who fired?"

"Of course it was. Did you not have a weapon? Monsieur Martin certainly made sure that the inside of the carriage was well-equipped." She nodded to the rear of the carriage where the fellow to her pistol sat mounted in a holster secured to the wall.

"I was equipped with a weapon but without the skill to use it."

"Have you never fired a pistol? I thought you lived in Derbyshire. They must have pheasants there."

"Only a handful of times, not enough to be confident of hitting my mark from a careening carriage." It had never bothered Gyles before that he was not a crack shot, but for some reason, at this moment he felt hopelessly inadequate. He had thrust himself on Louisa Lymington to ensure her safety, and she had proven herself far more capable of taking care of herself than he was.

"Perhaps I ought to let you ride inside the coach," said Louisa cuttingly, "for your own protection."

"That won't be necessary," said Gyles, his cheeks flaming with embarrassment.

"Still determined to be a pebble in my shoe?" Louisa arched an eyebrow. She climbed out of the coach, pushed past Gyles, and approached the driver. "*Merci beaucoup* for your fine driving, *monsieur*." She sent a meaningful look at Gyles. "I think those gentlemen of the road will think twice about accosting your coach again."

The laconic man tipped his hat to her, and Gyles caught a whiff of onions.

Later that night, as they were bedding down in the stables, Jacques approached Gyles. "Monsieur," he said gruffly. "My English is poor, but you claim to be *un valet de pied, n'est-ce pas?*"

"A footman?" guessed Gyles.

"*Oui*, but I think you are more than a…footman," Jacques said gruffly.

"I'm not sure why you think that," said Gyles cautiously. He shrugged his shoulders to shake off the straw sticking to his back. He did not particularly enjoy sleeping rough in the stables without a featherbed but he would not complain.

"And," continued Jacques. "I think you are less than a man." He thrust a short pistol in Gyles' direction along with a pouch of powder and shot. "You must become one."

"Arms make the man?" Gyles combed a hand through his chestnut hair.

"*Le bon Dieu* makes the man," said the coachman with a grunt. "*Le bon Dieu* and practise, Monsieur Pebble. I will teach you tomorrow, before we leave."

"Thank you," said Gyles, accepting the gift with good grace and tucking it into his satchel. He would have to rise early indeed to shoot targets with Monsieur Martin before they left in the morning. But to someday earn the praise of Lady Louisa—it would be worth it.

CHAPTER TWENTY-SEVEN

Paris

THE TRIP TO PARIS took four days. As they came into the outskirts of Paris, the effects of the Revolution became even more apparent. Churches and abbeys, blackened by fire or half torn down by angry mobs littered the roads. Dilapidated ruin greeted them everywhere. And yet, for every ruin, a glistening new building project raised its head as they entered the capital proper. Napoleon was ready to resurrect the city from the ashes of what had come before.

Louisa, even though she had never been to Paris, had a good sense of how to establish herself in a foreign city. "Take me to *la Banque de France*," she instructed Jacques. Gyles waited outside the building while Louisa established a safe deposit for her jewellery and a line of credit that would allow her to lease *un hôtel* in the best area of town. It was not long before she exited the bank, a smile of triumph playing on her lips and a black moustached clerk trailing behind her ready to offer his services.

"Did they not ask for papers establishing who you are?" asked Gyles in a low voice.

"No," said Louisa, "they were happy to accommodate *la Comtesse Dammartin*. One would almost think they remembered my grandmother who held that title—although that is impossible. This bank did not exist ten years ago."

With the help of the agent from the bank, an obsequious fellow named Pierre Dupont, Louisa secured a townhouse near the *Champs-Élysées*. It was fully furnished with everything from couches to clocks, and the elegant columns flanking the entrance proclaimed it a place of quality. "I shall also need to employ some servants."

"*Bien sûr, madame,*" said Monsieur Dupont, twirling his black moustache with one hand. "*Un chef,* a housekeeper, a lady's maid, two housemaids, and a coachman." He looked at Gyles' tall frame and broad shoulders. "A second footman would not go amiss, but I guarantee you will not find a matched pair for this one, *eh bien?*"

"No, I suppose not," said Louisa, seeing Gyles through the Frenchman's appreciative eyes. It was true that the English usually had the advantage of the French in height and breadth. It was also true that Mr. Audeley was an impressive specimen for even an Englishman. The green breeches clung tightly to his muscular thighs and his calves filled out the grey stockings to perfection. If only he need not wear that ridiculous, old-fashioned wig that was *de rigeur* for footmen!

With Monsieur Dupont's able assistance, the house was soon staffed with Monsieur Broussard presiding in the kitchen, Madame Laurent overseeing the establishment, and Cosette Boucher attending to the mistress with her hair and gowns.

Louisa elected *not* to secure a second footman. What need was there when her original footman was so assiduous to please?

You just don't like the idea of going out in your carriage without Gyles Audeley trailing after you. Are you that dependent on him? Do you need him so badly?

No, she did *not* need him, Louisa told herself, but all the same, since he refused to return to London, she really ought to buy him some new livery. The day after she visited the modiste to commission her own gowns, she gave Gyles the card for a tailor and told him to get his measurements taken.

"I've decided I don't like that silver and green you keep wearing. This is not Lord Kendall's house. The house of Dammartin has its own colours." She did not tell Gyles that she had invented them the previous day to sort well with his brown eyes and chestnut hair. When Gyles went to visit the tailor, he would find himself fitted for two suits of dark navy with bronze buttons.

"If I might be so bold," said Gyles, taking the card for the tailor and turning it over in his hand to examine it, "I think I would like to visit the cobbler first."

Louisa looked down at his feet, crammed into silver-buckled shoes that looked half an inch too small. "Of course," she said, sensing the discomfort he must feel simply while standing still. She shook her head in disbelief. "Have you really been wearing those all this time?"

Gyles gave a shrug. "There was no time to make a change."

Louisa did not think that any other gentleman of her acquaintance would have met that trial with such equanimity. She could only imagine how Uncle Nigel would howl to have shoes that pinched his toes so tightly. Her father would have sacked his valet if an alternate pair had not been located immediately.

"Of course, you must go to the cobbler right away, and you must have the bill sent here."

A brisk knock sounded on the door of the townhouse.

"But first, a visitor," said Gyles. He opened the door, and Louisa heard a suave male voice inquire whether *la Comtesse Dammartin* was *chez soi*.

From the hallway, she heard Gyles say, "Pardon me. Wait a moment," and then shut the door in the visitor's face.

"I couldn't understand a word of that," he said sheepishly.

"Then you had better stop answering the door," said Louisa tartly. "Show the fellow in. He's asking for me. I'm curious to find out who it could be."

Gyles opened the door and gestured for the visitor to enter. A man of medium height with curly black corkscrew hair strutted into the room as if he were a peacock at a menagerie. The shoulders of his purple striped cutaway tailcoat were padded out to an enormous width, and his buff pantaloons were so tight as to leave little of his lower half to the imagination.

He stopped in place when he saw Louisa observing him from the hallway and struck a pose. Then, he pulled out a monocle and looked her up and down appraisingly.

"Who, sir, are you?" demanded Louisa.

"Alphonse Aubert, *le Comte Dammartin*. And you, I take it, must be my wife."

CHAPTER TWENTY-EIGHT

The Count

GYLES UNDERSTOOD LITTLE OF the conversation between Louisa and their dandyish visitor, but the name Dammartin was easy enough to decipher. Had Louisa accidentally claimed a title that already belonged to someone else?

The conversation grew louder and more heated until finally, the ridiculous popinjay rushed forward, seized Louisa's hands, and deposited kisses on both of her cheeks. Then the two of them retired to the drawing room to continue their conversation while Gyles was left standing at attention in the entrance hall.

His mouth fell open in disbelief. The urgent visit to the cobbler was forgotten; the new livery could be put off till another day. He resolved to maintain a watchful presence at the house until this interloper took himself off to Jericho or somewhere even warmer.

"Did you understand what they said?" asked a pert voice in heavily accented English.

Gyles looked up and saw that Louisa's new lady's maid, Cosette Bouchard, had been eavesdropping from the top of the stairs. She was pretty, petite, and polished, with the expressive eyes and elegant nose that characterised so many Frenchwomen. She might have been twenty-five years old. She might have been thirty. It was impossible to tell.

"Not much," Gyles admitted.

"Come, I will tell you what they say."

Cosette sat down on the highest step of the staircase. Gyles ascended the stairs two at a time till he came to the top and sat down beside her.

"*He* is the Comte Dammartin. He accuses your lady of masquerading as his wife."

"I'm sure she meant to do no such thing—"

"*Eh bien,* how quick you are to defend her." Cosette looked at him slyly. "You know her well, I think."

"I have been serving her for over four years," said Gyles. It was true. One could say that he had entered her service long ago at Carlton House and never given up the position. And he knew her as well as anyone could know Louisa Lymington, which was to say, not well at all. The walls she built against all intruders were so high that he wondered if a man could ever scale them. He had made some headway, but he did not flatter himself that he had reached the top.

Sharp-sighted Cosette, however, had sensed that there was something more to Gyles and Louisa's relationship than mistress and footman. "Your lady says she did not steal the name, that she inherited it from her mother."

Gyles nodded. That would make sense. Louisa's mother had been a Frenchwoman who had married the Duke of Warrenton.

No doubt she had assumed her family's title when she had fled to England, bringing the family fortune in her coffers.

"But *le comte,* he says that is impossible. He says that the title was—how do you say it?—defunct. It is only in the last year that our emperor has brought it back to life."

"So Napoleon awarded the title of Comte Dammartin to this dandy?"

"*Oui,* he did the emperor a great service." Cosette laughed. "Or so he says."

"Why did Napoleon choose that particular title?"

"Ah, that is a good question, Monsieur Pebble. *Le comte* says that it belonged to his grandfather before the Revolution. Your lady, she objects. She says it belonged to *her* grandfather. And then they realise the truth and begin to fall on each other's necks and kiss." Cosette looked at Gyles archly to see if *he* had realised the truth of the matter yet. "They are cousins, *monsieur.* Their mothers were sisters. Their grandfather, the old *comte,* was one and the same!"

Gyles took a deep breath. Cousins! So, Louisa did have family in France. His brow furrowed. Somehow, that fact did not entirely please him, especially if her family was this fancy-frocked Frenchman who was entirely too free with his kisses. Gyles knew enough of the aristocratic classes to realise that a cousin was often a favoured option for a matrimonial partner.

"What do you think they are saying to each other now in the drawing room?"

"*Sacrebleu.*" Cosette touched his arm playfully. "Who knew the English could be so jealous? I must teach you French, *monsieur,* so you can spy on your lady better."

"That would be...useful," said Gyles. He could not completely deny interest in "his lady" when Mademoiselle Bouchard was able to see right through him. "I'd be much obliged to you for lessons."

"What will you say first? *'Je t'adore!'*" Cosette batted her long eyelashes at him and pursed her lips.

"I think there's time enough to learn that later," said Gyles, fully able to guess what those words meant. "First, you must teach me how to answer the door in French, for I'm afraid I shall embarrass us all if I can't understand milady's guests."

——

Louisa laughed until her stomach and the sides of her face hurt. Cousin Alphonse was such a ridiculous creature. He was like a tropical parrot at an eccentric dowager's home—one never knew what perch he would fly to, how long he would preen himself, or what absurdity he would next proclaim.

"You can imagine my surprise, *cherie*," he said, sitting down on the drawing room sofa and reaching for her hand. "I go away for two weeks for a house party at Malmaison, and when I come back, I find that I have a wife. *Sacrebleu!* What have I done? At first, I think these rumour-mongers must be lying. And then I think, how much champagne did I consume at the gambling hell before I left Paris? What delightful ladybird did I meet while in my cups? And which of my servants was stupid enough to summon a priest to read the vows when I stumbled home? I have a *comtesse*? But who?"

The purple-coated popinjay released her hand, jumped to his feet, and began to stride about the room. "'She is English,' they tell me. English! But I have never been to England. 'She is beautiful,' they say. I would hope so! Even with too much champagne in his head, *le Comte Dammartin* would not marry a cow of a woman. 'And she is very tall.'"

The count drew himself up to his full height. "Tall! *That* is what worries Alphonse most of all. She is tall! What does this mean? Will I have to add heels to all my boots? Will I have to shorten the legs of her chair so that her head is not higher than mine?" He paused. "But then I think to myself, no. Napoleon's new wife is taller than he, and it matters to no one. No one will laugh at Alphonse Aubert if his wife is tall."

"I am pleased to hear that my height is not an insuperable impediment," said Louisa, trying to keep her expression neutral.

"Yes, and now that I see you, your height is *très charmante*. You are not a gatepost like I feared but a goddess." He leaned down, seized her hand, and raised it to his lips. "I catch a glimpse of you, and I am content with the idea that you are my wife. But then, I find you are not my wife at all, but my cousin. *Ma grande et jolie cousine anglaise*!" He perched on the sofa beside her, careful not to bend too quickly in his tight pantaloons. "Why is it that you have come to France, *cherie*?"

Louisa smiled. She might enjoy her cousin's theatrics, but she was not about to share her predicament with him. "I have always wanted to visit the land of my mother."

"But in wartime! *Comme c'est difficile*." He looked at her quizzically. "How did you persuade your papa to let you come?"

"My father died two years ago."

"Then who is your guardian, *ma petite*? Never tell me that so beautiful a young woman is alone in the world!" He looked most eager as he said the last, as if he hoped that such a thing might be the case.

"Not alone, exactly." Louisa deflected the question. "But I am fully able to handle my own affairs." She adopted a business-like tone and began to move the conversation in a direction of her own choosing. "And I am delighted to have made your acquaintance, Alphonse. How fortuitous it is! You must introduce me to proper society in Paris."

"*Mais oui,* I shall," said her cousin obligingly. "But first I must tell my mistresses that the rumours are false. I did not wed an Englishwoman while in my cups. It is *ma cousine* who has come to Paris and played a grand joke on us all."

"Mistresses!" echoed Louisa. "Do you have more than one?"

"Occasionally," said Alphonse, pursing his lips. "Lately, yes. But sometimes they fight so much, I must say farewell to one of them. And then there are tears, many tears, and in the end, I always take the banished one back again." He beamed at Louisa. "But when they learn I am not married, they shall both be *très contentes* for at least a fortnight. Although, perhaps I ought not to tell them, for when I came home from Malmaison, the fighting had stopped and they were fully united in hatred of you."

"I am glad to have done you such a service, cousin," said Louisa, rising from the sofa and giving Alphonse her hand to kiss once again. They walked together toward the open door of the drawing room. "Pebble," said Louisa, looking about the entryway. "Will you show *le comte* out?"

"Yes, milady," said Gyles, his voice trailing down from the floor above. His cheeks were pink as he descended the stairs, and Louisa wondered what he had been doing up there. Her eyes travelled up the bannister, and she saw the swinging skirts of her lady's maid heading down the upstairs corridor.

Gyles cleared his throat. "I would be delighted to show him the door." He opened the door and clicked his heels together. "*Adieu, mon seigneur.*"

Louisa looked at him sharply. A week ago, he had known nothing of French. Was he truly making an effort to learn her language?

You make too much of it. What are a few words? He may understand how to say good-bye, but he will never understand you. Make no mistake about that.

CHAPTER TWENTY-NINE

Society

Louisa discovered that Alphonse was only too happy to announce his *cousine Anglaise* to polite society in Paris. The next day, invitations to card parties and *soirées* began to arrive, all of them located along the expensive Rue du Faubourg Saint Honoré. Louisa agreed to accompany Alphonse to an exclusive salon in two weeks' time. She hoped fervently that her modiste would finish her new gowns by then.

When she placed her order, Madame Ballesdens, the modiste, had recommended the sheer white muslins that were popular among Parisienne ladies. This recommendation had given Louisa pause. She had avoided the colour white ever since her unfortunate encounter with the Earl of Yarmouth at Carlton House. That had proven something of a difficulty, for white was a standard colour for young ladies; however, for her debut in London, she had satisfied the expectations of the ton by wearing primrose pink and a delicate sky blue. Now, she decided to give up pastels altogether and opted for solid gowns in deep amethyst, rich burgundy, and bottle green.

Although she refused to wear the popular sheer fabrics, she was determined not to be a dowd. The contours of her new gowns were based on the latest French fashion plates, and the necklines were much more daring than those she had worn in London. Madame Ballesdens assured her that to show one's decolletage was *de rigeur.* The Empress Josephine—whom everyone knew was far more alluring than Napoleon's new Austrian empress—regularly revealed most of her bosom.

On the day of the salon, Louisa told her maid Cosette to have a bath drawn in her room. She did not remember that the hot water would be carried up the stairs by none other than her faithful footman. Louisa's cheeks flamed red as she sat in her dressing gown by her mirror and watched Gyles pour steaming bucket after steaming bucket into the copper tub. She avoided his eye. Somehow, the thought of him handling her bathing water was too indecent for words.

But you must remember that you refused to engage a second footman. Surely, you knew that this would throw you further into Gyles Audeley's company?

"Will that be all, milady?" asked Gyles. A little of the water had sloshed onto the front of his new livery, but the dark navy colour hid that admirably. He had taken off his powdered wig since he was not receiving visitors at the door, and his chestnut hair was damp and ruffled from the steam.

"Yes, that is quite enough," said Louisa brusquely, trying to get rid of the handsome Mr. Pebble as soon as possible. She detected a mischievous smile on Cosette's face as the maid feigned busyness at the door of the open wardrobe.

Gyles touched his forelock as he left the room without a word. As soon as he shut the door, Cosette closed the wardrobe. She helped Louisa disrobe and climb into the bath.

"*La*," said Cosette, "I wonder you can keep from staring at Monsieur Pebble in his new livery. Madame Laurent was forced to chase the maids from the neighbouring house away from our window, for they cannot help but stop and stare when Monsieur Pebble has his sleeves rolled up polishing the silver."

"Can they not?" said Louisa, filled with an unreasonable sense of pique. She could not tell whether it was the thought of Gyles' taut forearms or the insolence of the neighbour's servants that gave her the most discomfort.

"But perhaps *all* the gentlemen in England are this handsome, *eh bien*?" Cosette's tone was coy. "Perhaps all the footmen and gentlemen across the Channel are tall and handsome and charming...."

"No, far from it," said Louisa, grudgingly admitting the truth of it to both Cosette and to herself. Gyles was one of the most handsome men she had ever met. Handsomer than Uncle Nigel and Cousin Alphonse. Handsomer by far than any of the five men who had paid her court during her season as the Incomparable.

"Ah, well, it is good that you shall leave him home tonight when you go out with *le comte*, so that *le comte* is not too jealous." Cosette gave a mischievous grin. "Do not fear. Madame Laurent and I, we shall keep him safe from the housemaids."

Somehow, the idea of Gyles spending a cosy evening at home with Cosette Bouchard was as distasteful as sour milk to Louisa, but as she was not riding in her own carriage, she had no need for Gyles to escort her.

Why can you not put Gyles Audeley out of your head? Your cousin Alphonse will introduce you to a host of cosmopolitan men tonight. Stop letting a provincial gardener from Derbyshire spin your mind around like a whirligig.

Despite her admonitions to herself, Louisa continued to be distracted in mind. She dried herself beside the fire, and then Cosette attired her in shift and stays, laced up her bottle green evening gown, and coiffed her honey-gold hair. "Monsieur Dupont delivered the jewellery you requested," said Cosette, retrieving a case in the wardrobe.

"*Bien,*" said Louisa. She had instructed the agent from the bank to sell her most expensive diamond necklace to finance her mounting expenses, but to bring another of the pieces to her house. Her mother's emeralds would still be brilliant enough to draw appreciative stares.

When Cosette had finished with her, she brought out a looking glass for Louisa's approval. Louisa stared. The pastel debutante from last season was gone, and in her place was a supremely elegant and supremely confident lady of fashion. She could have graced the arm of the highest-ranking man in France. She could have been the hostess for the most exclusive salon in Paris. The emeralds glittered alluringly on a curvaceous canvas of creamy skin.

Cousin Alphonse came to the door, fashionably late. Louisa was already downstairs in the entry hall, calling for her cloak as the footman admitted her escort.

"Ah, my *comtesse,*" said Alphonse with a smirk, brushing past Gyles. He kissed the back of her gloved hand and then added several kisses to her cheeks for good measure. Taking Louisa's gloved hand, he lifted his arm high and spun her around in an allemande, observing her figure from every angle. "*Très magnifique*. Shall we depart?"

Louisa nodded at Gyles. He took the velvet cloak Cosette was holding and draped it about her shoulders. She felt the tips of his fingers brush her collarbone as he settled it in place. That accidental graze sent a fire through her veins that all of Alphonse's kisses had failed to kindle. Louisa turned her head and saw Gyles's eyes studiously avoiding her face, or indeed, any part of her. Had he felt it too?

She adjusted the velvet cloak to cover her half-exposed bosom and took her cousin's arm. It was stiff from the dark wool coat he wore but not as firm as the support Gyles often lent her.

They exited the door into the cold evening air, but as Alphonse was handing her up into the carriage, she was acutely aware that her servants had come out onto the chilly porch and were watching them take their leave. "Do you like milady's new gown?" she overheard Cosette say.

"No," her footman replied. His voice was taut with some emotion—displeasure, no doubt.

"Oh, Monsieur Pebble," said Cosette with a laugh. She tapped a pert finger against Gyles' nose. "You are so severe. I daresay you dislike my gown as well." She pulled her shoulders back and thrust her bosom forward. Gyles blushed, and Cosette began to laugh.

Louisa bristled as she watched this display from out the carriage window.

What does it matter if Cosette flirts with him? He is not bound to you in any way. Have you not told him repeatedly that you do not want him and that he should return home?

Alphonse, on the seat beside her, reached out and pressed her gloved hand. He was magnificently attired in a red silk waistcoat and a coat of black superfine that matched his curls. A ruby stickpin glittered in his snowy white cravat, and he looked like the hero of a Drury Lane stage play. "Are you ready for tonight, *ma cherie?* You will dazzle all of Paris with your emerald fire!"

Louisa forced a smile. "If you do not blind them first with all your elegance, *mon cousin*."

He lifted her hand and kissed it, his flamboyant gesture framed by the carriage window, before they rolled away along the cobblestones to the Rue du Faubourg Saint Honoré.

CHAPTER THIRTY

Letter

THE NEXT DAY GYLES' eyes were tired as a factory worker's. He had not been able to sleep until the Comte Dammartin's carriage returned Louisa halfway through the night. And then, after that, he had tossed and turned on his pallet in the servants' quarters until the cock's crow. It was none of his business how cosy Louisa chose to be with her cousin, but he could not trust the fellow and liking him was out of the question.

Louisa stayed late abed. Then she breakfasted in her room. Cosette, who had attended to her mistress when she returned home, informed Gyles that milady's appearance at the salon had been a triumph. Every man there had been eating out of her hand.

Gyles spent the morning in a foul mood. Why had he even come to Paris with Louisa Lymington? Far from being on the fringes of the French elite, she had fallen on her feet like a cat into the cream of Parisian society. Her cousin might be a danger to her, but it was a danger that Louisa was courting.

Gyles thought of all that he had left behind to come here—his mother, his writings, his transplanted rosebush. He had not even given instruction for how to care for it, and now it was no doubt withering away in the Kendall House carriage yard.

"Cosette," he asked, "how do I post a letter in Paris?"

"A letter?" said Cosette, her little ears burning with curiosity. "And to whom would Monsieur Pebble be writing?"

"Home," said Gyles vaguely. He listened attentively as Cosette explained where the nearest post-house stood. *"Merci beaucoup."*

"Voilà!" she said proudly. "You will speak French like a Frenchman before I have done with you."

After he had finished the chores that Madame Laurent set for him, Gyles sat down to write a quick note. He blotted it, sealed it, and then headed out of doors.

"Where to, Monsieur Pebble?" asked Jacques, pulling his pipe from his mouth as Gyles walked past the carriage house. As the only two male servants of the house, they shared the quarters above the stables. Gyles had become as close to the quiet coachman as was reasonable for an English gentleman and a French domestic.

"The post-house."

Unlike Cosette, Jacques had no questions about the identity of Gyles' correspondent and uttered only a single comment about the inadequacy of the French mail system. "Don't expect a quick response."

"Aye, I imagine the blockade stops most ships from moving between our ports." Gyles did not understand the complete politics of shipping, but he hoped that since he had been able to travel between Plymouth and Morlaix, a letter might be able to travel the return route.

Jacques nodded toward the carriage. "First, I take you to the post-house. Then, we go shooting."

"No, no, I'll walk," said Gyles, declining the offer. They had gone shooting half a dozen times now, in a half-frozen field outside the city, and still there was no noticeable improvement in Gyles' aim. Perhaps he was destined to be a poor shot.

Jacques grunted and went back to oiling the harness. He had allowed Lady Louisa to paint her own Dammartin coat-of-arms on the doors of his coach, but the vehicle and the horses still belonged to him, and he prided himself on keeping it in prime condition. The air had turned bitter cold this morning as the season of winter neared. Gyles rubbed his hands together as he walked, keeping a brisk pace to keep the blood flowing through his limbs. He wondered how cold it was across the Channel at Kendall House in the courtyard where his rosebush sat.

At the post-house, he delivered his letter to the attendant, and then turned to hurry back to the *Champs-Élysées.* His step was arrested, however, when he caught sight of a Frenchman he knew. It was Monsieur Dupont, with his curling black moustache, the agent from the bank whom Louisa had engaged to manage her affairs. Dupont shifted his weight from foot to foot as he waited in the square, no doubt even colder than Gyles as he did not have the benefit of brisk movement to warm himself. Gyles almost saluted the man out of instinct but caught himself in time. A footman had no place greeting those above him in society.

Before he passed by, he saw someone else salute Monsieur Dupont, however. It was the Comte Dammartin, pink as a tulip in a primrose coat, mincing across the cobblestones in his skin-tight buff pantaloons. Monsieur Dupont's face lit up to see the count, and the two men disappeared into a nearby eating house.

Gyles frowned. How peculiar that Louisa's agent should also be a colleague of her cousin. Perhaps the bank dealt in the new house of Dammartin's money as well? Or perhaps the meeting stemmed solely from their mutual connection with Louisa?

Gyles was aware that he did not have the skills to eavesdrop on fluent French-speakers, even if he was surreptitious enough to enter the eating house undetected. He could pursue the matter no further at this moment. He had no intention, however, of forgetting this coincidence, and it gave him an even greater suspicion and dislike of Louisa's dandified cousin.

He hurried home, wondering if Louisa would be awake and needing anything from him. Despite her chilly exterior and seeming lack of gratitude, he was almost certain that she felt his presence as keenly as he felt hers. Last night, when he had placed the cloak about her shoulders, a finely tuned frisson of awareness had passed through both of them. No matter how fiercely she scorned his help, she was not immune to him. He had seen her breath catch in her throat as his fingers brushed against her neck, and it had taken all his willpower not to stare at her in that voluptuous bottle-green dress.

Fool though he might be, he would stay in Paris as long as she needed him. Even if the blockade that she had placed around her heart never lifted. Even if the wall surrounding her affections was always impossible to climb.

CHAPTER THIRTY-ONE

Quarrel

"Where is Monsieur Pebble?" demanded Louisa. She had dressed for the day—in a striking patterned gown of plum and gold—and descended the staircase of her Paris townhouse to decide her next course of action.

Last night had been...decadent. Cousin Alphonse had displayed her like a prized English flower to a room full of colonels and generals and *comtes* and courtesans. The champagne had flowed freely, and every time she turned around, she heard men saying, "Dammartin, you must introduce me to *ta cousine.*" And, in response, she had smiled, and sparkled, and scintillated like a cut diamond.

Yet, despite the splendour of it all, the whole evening had felt vapid, as if it were missing some vital spark to make the moment come alive, to make the moment mean something. For Louisa was certain that, despite all the lilting laughter and lively banter, no one truly *meant* anything they said at this exclusive salon. It was as vacuous a set as her father had befriended, just like Prince George's cronies at Carlton House.

She reminded herself that the importance of the evening had been less in the conversation than in the connections. If she could successfully make her *entrée* into Parisian society, she would have an acceptable position to wait out the rest of the year until she reached her majority. Rather than hiding in the shadows as a governess, she could enjoy this season as an Incomparable without fear of Uncle Nigel or Mr. Digby. In five months' time, she would be a free woman, with no guardian to dictate commands and no husband to fritter away her wealth. Then she could decide whether to stay in Paris or return to London on her own terms.

The success she met at the salon came with its own disadvantages. She had a headache from the champagne, and she barely remembered the carriage ride home in Alphonse's company. She had one niggling memory of pushing him away when he tried to sit too close. She did not think he had taken any further liberties, but she was determined she would not drink again in his company. Her head ached as a reminder of her imprudence, but it was not so bad that she had to keep to her bed. That was a blessing, for if she stayed in her chambers, she would not catch sight of the one person she was most curious to see....

Sweeping through the entrance hall in her morning dress of plum and gold, Louisa noticed that her liveried footman was absent from his place. "Where is Monsieur Pebble?"

"He went to the post, milady," said Cosette, bobbing a curtsey.

The post! Who do you think he is writing to? Is he sending letters home to England? To Penelope Trafford? To your uncle, the duke?

Louisa's face turned into a rigid mask. "Do you know the name of his correspondent?"

Cosette smiled, a perfect smile with dimples. "*La!* He did not say." She gave her employer an arch look. "I do not think it was a lady, though."

"I do not pay you to make insinuations," said Louisa, her patience exhausted with Cosette's unwelcome suggestions. The maid was proficient at laundering her clothes and coiffing her hair, but her impudence was unmatched.

"Of course not, milady," said Cosette, bobbing another curtsey with a contrite expression.

It was at that moment that Gyles entered the hallway, having come upstairs from the kitchen.

"Monsieur Pebble," said Louisa sharply.

"Milady." He bowed, his trim navy livery both eminently attractive and a constant reminder of his current position. Louisa remembered when their positions were reversed, when she had owed *him* the deference due to a gentleman while she was dressed in the drab dove-grey of a governess. Would they ever meet each other on an equal plane when neither of them was playing a masquerade?

"I need to speak with you. Privately." Louisa nodded for Gyles to follow her into the drawing room, and then—ignoring Cosette's gaping mouth—shut the door firmly behind them.

"Well?" she demanded as Gyles relaxed his posture. Apparently, he felt more at ease in her presence when it was just the two of them alone. "Where were you?"

"I had an errand."

"My footmen do not go on errands unless I send them."

"So, you consider me your footman now?" He crossed his arms and leaned against the white-panelled drawing room wall. "I recall you dismissing me from your service."

"Then you also recall me paying for your livery when you refused to leave. Of course, you are my footman. What was your errand?"

"I had a letter to send."

"You had no right." Louisa felt her words begin to come faster. Her heart beat like the footsteps of a link boy running downhill, and her violet-brown eyes opened like moonflowers in the dark. "What did you tell him? Did you say I was in Paris?"

He knows where you are now. He will come to find you, with that big-bellied Mr. Digby on his coattails, and they'll spirit you away to—

Before she knew it, Gyles' hands had reached out to place themselves on her shaking shoulders. "Nothing. I told him nothing." His voice was soothing, understanding, consoling. "The letter was not to your uncle."

"Then, to whom?" demanded Louisa, regaining control of herself. "To Miss Trafford?"

Gyles' hands dropped slowly to his sides. "Certainly not. I have no understanding with Penelope Trafford."

Louisa took a deep breath and attempted to deflect attention from her own shocking display of feeling. "She likes you—it is obvious. You've awakened expectations by spending time with her."

Gyles' brown eyes considered her face. "I've spent far more time with another young lady. Yet somehow, I doubt that expectations have been awakened in that quarter."

Louisa blanched.

What is this? A warning to keep your own expectations in check? A piece of advice not to see anything in his pursuit of you beyond an impartial display of chivalry?

"If not to my uncle or Miss Trafford, then to whom, sir? To your mother?"

"It probably ought to have been. But no, it was to Sir Abraham Hume."

Louisa frowned. "Who is that? I've heard the name before—"

"He is a botanist. I asked him to look in on my rosebush at Kendall House."

Louisa stared at him blankly. He had gone to the post for a rosebush?

He gave her a crooked smile, as if he were embarrassed to have brought up the matter. His chagrin made him look even more boyish and more charming than usual.

"Your rosebush! Upon my word, Mr. Audeley, you are a very singular fellow."

"I am sorry if my peculiarities give you a distaste of me."

"Not a...distaste," said Louisa, feeling as self-conscious as she had been when Gyles had delivered her bathwater. "Simply a bewilderment."

Truth be told, her bewilderment was more about his memory than his peculiarities. Did he even remember their previous encounter at Carlton House? She decided to explore the matter and give him an opening. "Why do you care so much about roses?"

"I have a large rose garden in Derbyshire," Gyles explained patiently. "I am a rose collector, and the rose I brought with me to London is one of my rarest. I left it, rather suddenly if you remember, and I'm afraid it might not be getting along satisfactorily on its own."

"You are a rosarian," said Louisa, remembering when he had taught her the word four and a half years ago.

Clearly, he has no memory of your first conversation, or he would not have spent so long explaining himself. No doubt Gyles Audeley helps every woman who comes across his path, and he's helped so many of them that he does not even remember the deed. He has no particular fondness for you—he only followed you to France to ensure your safety as any chivalrous gentleman would have done.

"Yes, I am a rosarian," repeated Gyles, oblivious to the conversation going on inside her head. "I hope to write a book one day, collating the things I have learned throughout my endeavours in gardening."

"A book?" Louisa could think of nothing more tedious, and yet somehow, he made the topic interesting because he was so...interested. She felt herself leaning in closer to him, the smell of freshly laundered linen coming from the neckcloth about his throat.

"On the cultivation and care of the *rosa rubiginosa*." He looked down modestly. "I beg your pardon. I suppose I must seem insufferably pedantic."

Louisa made no answer. Pedantic, certainly. But somehow, not insufferable. And yet, how much he must be suffering to leave his garden and his writings behind to follow her across the continent! How had she ever allowed him to do it? *That* was the insufferable thing.

"Mr. Audeley," she said, taking a deep breath. "The more I know about you, the more I am certain that it was a mistake for you to leave England. You should tend to your roses yourself. Go home, sir."

At that, her tall, broad-shouldered footman looked her in the eye. "With all due respect, milady, no. I won't leave your side until I'm certain you're safe and secure."

"My *preux chevalier*," said Louisa, her lip curling scornfully.

Your white knight. If it takes scorn to send him home where he belongs, then scorn is what you must give him.

"Your *preux chevalier*," replied Gyles, and there was nothing mild-mannered about the glittering fire in his brown eyes. "Will that be all, milady?"

"Yes. That will be all," said Louisa, dismissing him with a flick of the hand.

Chapter Thirty-Two

Invitation

THE NEXT SEVERAL WEEKS were a whirlwind of gaiety. Louisa had never spent such a festive Christmas season as she did in Paris, attending salons, rout parties, the opera, and balls. As a child, she had often spent a quiet Yuletide at home while her father disappeared to lavish house parties in a neighbouring county. When she had experienced London society last year, the season had started after the festivities of Christmas. Now, for the first time, she could experience the grandeur of Christmas in town, the flamboyantly magical town of Paris.

Even more festive than Christmas was the French New Year. The Revolutionaries had tried to do away with it, creating a new calendar that shifted the start of the year to harvest time. But Napoleon, when he had taken the French government by storm, had upended the calendar as well. No more of these ten-day weeks and Friday-faced festivals. It was back to a proper New Year in France, and, having been deprived of it for so many years, the people celebrated it with even more jollity.

New Year led into January, and by then, Louisa had firmly established herself as the novelty of Parisien society. After a particularly late night queening it over a literary salon, she slept late abed and then rose just in time to receive her cousin, the Comte Dammartin. It was an hour before the time that visitors were regularly admitted, but he claimed the privilege of a relative.

Dressed in a Grecian-inspired morning dress with brooches at the shoulders, Louisa received him in the drawing room. She was so tired from all her late-night frivolity that she could barely keep from yawning as he made a leg and greeted her with his characteristic enthusiasm.

"Ah, *ma cousine*, you must allow me to congratulate you. Everyone is talking about the Lady Louisa."

"*Vraiment?* What are they saying?"

"That you are an Englishwoman with the spirit of a French-woman. The Général Archambeau says he's never tasted such spice served in a saucer of cream." Alphonse kissed his fingers and fanned them at her. "You were magnificent!"

"You are too kind to me," said Louisa. "If you go on with such flattery, I shall be so puffed up I will want to host my own salon."

"And the crowds would flock to it!" Alphonse replied with enthusiasm. "But you must not set yourself up as a hostess just yet, *ma cherie*. I have a special treat in store for you next week."

"What sort of treat?" Louisa watched Alphonse's black corkscrew curls bounce in jubilation. Her own honey-gold hair would never curl that tightly, no matter how artfully her maid used the curling tongs.

"A house party. At Malmaison. There will be dinners and dancing—a masquerade ball!"

"Malmaison? Were you not just there two months ago? That is where Empress Josephine lives, *eh bien?*"

"*Oui,* I was visiting her when I heard of your arrival in Paris. She is a great friend of mine. Whenever she has guests to her chateau, she invites the Comte Dammartin. Next week, she bids me come again, for a fortnight this time."

"But surely your mistresses will miss you?"

"Have I not told you? *Eh bien,* you will laugh when you hear." Alphonse cleared his throat. "They have left me. *Non,* rather, I have sent them away."

"Which is it?"

"The latter. I told Hortense, no more. But what do you think happened? When I gave Hortense her *congé,* Mireille was so *furieuse* that she packed her things as well. And now they have taken rooms together by the Place de la Concorde, and both of them are abusing me to anyone who will listen."

"It sounds as if you mistreated them," said Louisa suspiciously.

"*Mais non!* How could you think it of me? I am a little forgetful perhaps. I do not care so much for them when I am busy with *ma jolie cousine*. Mireille, she asks me for jewellery. Hortense, she asks me for new gowns. Mireille desires a carriage. And Hortense, she asks me to go to Malmaison." Alphonse jumped to his feet and began to shake his finger with exasperation. "But that is too far. She knows I will bring *ma cousine* with me. I tell her no. I tell her to pack her things and leave. And then Mireille takes Hortense's part, and they are united against me!" He massaged his temples with his well-manicured fingers. "Pardon my excitement, but you cannot imagine the noise they made."

Louisa raised her dark golden eyebrows. Her own father had conducted his affairs much more discreetly, and Uncle Nigel, for all his flirtations, never quite seemed to hook the lady he was fishing for. But they had never outright declared their interest in the ladies they pursued. Such goings-on were not talked of in polite society, or at least not to unmarried young ladies like herself.

Why had Alphonse dismissed his mistresses? Louisa began to wonder whether Alphonse had developed the wrong idea of their relationship. He had been squiring her about Paris for weeks as a cousinly duty, but in what capacity did he anticipate her attending the house party with him? She cleared her throat. "I am not sure that it would be proper for me to go to Malmaison with you without a chaperone."

"Proper?" Alphonse began to laugh. "Ah, *cousine*, you are *tres anglaise*. The English always worry about what is 'proper.' *Eh bien*, you are *ma cousine*, are you not?" He reached down for Louisa's hand and pressed it. "What could be more proper?"

Louisa stiffened as Alphonse began to caress her hand. There was something unsettling about the fact that this flibbertigibbet was now focusing his attentions on *her*. She was confident of her ability to manage men like Horatio Smythe, but Alphonse was still an enigma. He had proved useful in introducing her to Paris society. Yet her intuition warned her against putting herself under his care for a fortnight in a foreign location. "*La*, my schedule is so full now. I am not sure I shall be able to attend—"

"Oh, but you must! Josephine has heard of you. She asks particularly that I bring you." Alphonse sat down beside her, so close that he was almost sitting on the edge of her Grecian skirt. He looked at her pleadingly.

Louisa wondered what exactly the former empress had said. Could it be that she had told Alphonse not to come unless he could bring his celebrated cousin with him? That would explain why he was so insistent that she go to Malmaison with him.

Louisa dissected the word in her mind. Mal. Maison. *The evil house.* "What is it like at Malmaison? The name itself does not inspire confidence."

Alphonse laughed. "You think it a *bad* house? *Non, non,* it is nothing of the kind. It is *tres grand,* as one would expect of a lady who has been empress. All gold and silk inside. The wine is only the best. And even if the weather is not fine, there are gardens in glass houses big enough to promenade in. When she is not presiding at games and dinners, *La Josephine* loves her gardens."

"What kind of gardens?"

"Roses. There is always a new variety that she has planted or must have. And when she learns of it, she sends couriers across the world for it until she obtains it. It is an obsession. If she were not so charming, I would tire of her talking about her garden. And besides, the roses make me sneeze. *Eh bien,* I feel sick with the head cold when I am in her greenhouse. And she is constantly putting flowers in my face." His voice sailed into a feminine imitation of the empress. "'Smell this one, Phonsie, and this one too!' *Argh, beurk!*"

Louisa stilled, ignoring Alphonse's melodramatic motions of disgust. Roses. She knew another person for whom they were also an obsession, possibly even more so than for the Empress Josephine. A visit to Malmaison would be a dream come true for Gyles.

But why would you care about Gyles Audeley's dreams? You must think about your own interests first of all, and becoming over-familiar with Cousin Alphonse is not part of your plan. You've avoided Mr. Digby, thus far. Why become entangled with another man now?

Louisa quieted her inner voice and made up her mind. For Gyles to see the garden, it was worth the risk.

"How delightful! I have a great curiosity to see Empress Josephine's glass house. Perhaps you will tire of me talking as well, for I wish to know everything about this rose garden. I will come to Malmaison with you. But I warn you, I shall be bringing my maid and my footman."

"*Bien sûr,* I would assume a lady needs a maid, but surely I have footmen enough for my carriage?"

"I want *my* footman." Louisa forgot to diminish the intensity in her own voice. She forgot to adopt a tone of *ennui* and play the game that Parisians knew so well.

Alphonse's eyes narrowed. "*Pourquoi?* Is he your lover?"

Louisa gasped. "How absurd! No, he is my protector, my *garde du corps.* A lady alone in a strange country needs to be sure she will not be taken advantage of."

Your bodyguard? What a load of poppycock! Don't you remember how completely useless he was on the road to Paris? He might give the appearance of protection, but in reality, you are the one who takes care of yourself—like you always have.

"But you have my protection." Alphonse looked at her from beneath veiled eyelids. His voice turned sultry and his mouth pursed into a sensual smile.

"I am not so sure I wish to be under your protection," said Louisa, forcing a laugh. This flirtation with the count was becoming dangerous, but the lure of a rare rose garden for Gyles to visit was too tantalising to resist. She could not explain it even to herself, but she knew that it was a gift she must give him.

Louisa rose from her seat. "I accept the invitation, *mon cousin.*"

As she and Alphonse passed out of the open door of the drawing room, she saw Gyles standing at attention in the hallway. She refused to meet his eye. It was a mercy that he spoke little French, for he had no doubt overheard every word that had passed between her and Alphonse.

Is he your lover?

Louisa felt her face colour at the remembrance of Alphonse's words. If her footman had understood anything, she hoped that it was merely the word for *roses.*

CHAPTER THIRTY-THREE

Journey

"*ALLONS, MES BEAUTÉS!*" SAID Jacques, leading out a pair of horses to attach to the traces of the carriage. "Come on, my beauties."

Gyles translated the words in his head without the need to think twice. His French lessons with Cosette had begun to bear fruit, and since the housekeeper, Madame Laurent, knew only French, he had become proficient at understanding his chores in that language.

The shooting lessons with Jacques, however, had been less of a triumph. No matter how much ball and powder they wasted, the practice seemed to have no effect. Gyles could dig a trench, or carry water, or polish silver with the best of them, but his shot always went wide whenever he pulled the trigger on a pistol.

After a dozen sessions of target practice on the outskirts of the town, the coachman had given up on him. "*Sacrebleu!* You'd best pray you have me with you if you meet a highwayman again," Jacques said gruffly. Then his enormous face split into an onion-scented grin, "Or Lady Louisa. She'll keep you safe."

It was the kind of friendly gibe that might make a man bristle, but Gyles found that he did not much mind. He liked the fact that Louisa could shoot a pistol—it was one less thing he had to worry about for her as she braved the world alone.

The road to Malmaison was not a long one, and it was unlikely that they would meet any highwaymen *en route*. Rumour had it that Napoleon still travelled the road often; he was unable to discard his affection for his first wife even as he busied himself trying to sire an heir on his second one. But Gyles had heard the count assure Louisa that Napoleon had not been invited to *this* house party.

As Jacques fastened the horses at the front of the carriage, Gyles hefted three trunks in swift succession onto the bench on the back. He took some rope from the carriage box and lashed them securely. From one trunk to three—from vanished heiress to enchantress of Paris—Lady Louisa had begun to grow into her new role.

Her wardrobe had expanded significantly leading up to the trip to Malmaison. Boxes had arrived from the modiste with a half dozen new slippers, shawls, morning gowns, evening gowns, and an elaborately embroidered ballgown in red and orange.

The black-moustached agent, Monsieur Dupont, had surfaced again, this time bearing three of Louisa's most sparkling sets of jewellery. After a consultation in the drawing room, he departed. Louisa had kept a parure of sapphires and returned the other pieces to Monsieur Dupont. Gyles heard the word *vendre* fluttering in the air, and from his French lessons with Cosette, he knew the word meant *to sell*.

How many of her jewels would Louisa need to sell? It was certainly difficult to finance the life of an aristocrat in Napoleon's Paris. Gyles wondered how long it would be before Louisa ran out of jewels to pawn. Presumably, she was hoping they would last until she came into her own inheritance a few months from now. That seemed to be her supreme goal: inheritance and independence. He had never needed to seek those things himself—they had been handed to him on the day his father died—but he admired her single-minded striving to take her life into her own hands and make something of it.

Whether that something would make her happy was another question altogether....

The reappearance of Monsieur Dupont reawakened the memory of the black-moustached man's meeting with the Comte Dammartin a month or more ago. Gyles did not know why it bothered him so much. Surely, a bank had many customers. Surely, it was only reasonable that an agent from the bank would meet with more clients than one. Surely, Dupont's conversation with the comte had nothing to do with Louisa. And yet, Gyles could not help feeling that Alphonse Aubert was a little too intentional with his attentions. Did he have some design on his cousin that involved the black-moustached bank agent?

It was a dozen miles from Paris to Malmaison. The count planned for Louisa's carriage, driven by Jacques Martin, to follow his own carriage at a close distance. But when Louisa heard the seating arrangements that put her alone with the count in the first carriage—and Gyles alone with Cosette in the second carriage—her heart-shaped face crinkled into a frown. "*Eh bien*, I shall need my maid beside me for the journey."

"Surely not," urged her cousin, a look of disappointment coming over his face.

"*Mais oui!* What if a curl were to come unpinned? I cannot exit the carriage at Malmaison with my hair looking like a stork's nest. I must have her with me to adjust my coiffure."

"*Certainement,* milady, "said Cosette, pertly inserting herself between Louisa and her cousin like a shell-knife between two halves of an oyster. Gyles grinned. The French maid was irrepressible and knew just how to tease her betters without landing herself in hot water.

"Oh, very well," said the count, blowing upwards to keep his black corkscrew curls from dangling in his eyes. It was an affectation that Gyles despised. He wished he had a pair of shears so that he could trim the count's overgrown forehead fringe like a garden hedge.

Gyles took Cosette's small trunk and added it to the luggage already secured. Jacques nodded at him as he walked past the horses. "You've lost both your ladies now," the coachman said gruffly, eyeing Cosette as she stood by Dammartin's carriage.

"Yes, but I'm not sure that either of them is truly mine."

"Hmm..." said the coachman, pulling out a pipe and filling it with tobacco. He looked at the pretty, petite lady's maid thoughtfully, his large face ruminating over something inscrutable.

"*Bon voyage,* Monsieur Pebble," called out Cosette, giving a saucy wink as she climbed into the count's conveyance. Gyles could not tell if the wink was for him or for Jacques.

"*Bon voyage,* Mademoiselle Bouchard," he replied. Removing his own satchel from his shoulder, he tossed it onto the seat in the carriage. He was about to climb in after it, but he paused to watch the count hand Louisa into the other coach.

Louisa dipped her head, adorned with a green and blue Toque Parée. The stylish cap framed her face to perfection with its edge of golden braid and plume of ostrich feathers.

"*Bon voyage,*" he said in the faintest whisper, doing little more than mouth the words. Her nostrils flared delicately. She turned her head away, and as her cousin stepped into the carriage after her, she disappeared from Gyles' sight.

The carriage ride to Malmaison took a little over two hours. Louisa could see that Alphonse was equally happy to flirt with either her or Cosette but that he was attempting to restrain himself from ogling the maid when he thought his cousin might be glancing in his direction.

Louisa rolled her eyes and looked out at the wintry countryside. What was it about men? Her father. Her uncle. Her cousin. They were all eyes and hands and other more unmentionable parts, but the one organ that seemed lamentably lacking in all of them was the heart. They were experts at flirtation but hopeless as King George's sons at any semblance of fidelity.

And then there was Gyles Audeley, steady as a draft horse, constant as a guide star, chivalrous as a knight tilting at windmills.

But also as unlikely as a parish priest to drop a flirtatious wink in your direction.

She thought he might have been saying something to her before she climbed into the carriage, but no doubt it was just some good-natured instruction to the carriage driver.

Louisa murmured a few absent-minded responses to Alphonse's sallies and continued to let her mind drift elsewhere.

She had a very good idea of what a proposal from her cousin would sound like, but what about one from Gyles Audeley? Would he stiffly enumerate the reasons for her suitability as her first suitor had done? Would he speculate that they ought to make a go of it like the inane Mr. Smythe? Or would he cover her arm and shoulder with kisses as she suspected Alphonse might do?

Surely, whatever form his declaration took, his behaviour would be perfectly proper throughout. She could not imagine that he would try to pull her into his arms. But at least he would not play the lecherous pig like the big-bellied Mr. Digby.

Louisa traced a fingertip against the condensation on the carriage window, ignoring Alphonse's foot brushing against Cosette's kid slipper on the carriage floor.

"Coquette" would be a better name for that minx. If she did not have such a way with your hair, you ought to consider dismissing her.

With her attention on the countryside, Louisa noticed immediately when the coachman veered off the main road to take the track to Malmaison. The wild woods opened up to a flowered meadow, and far in the distance was a grand chateau. Louisa was so taken with the perfect symmetry of the house that she failed to see something far more astonishing beyond the hedgerow.

"Milady!" said Cosette, clutching at Louisa's gloved arm. "Look!"

Louisa blinked to see a small horse, striped black and white, grazing in the rain on the other side of the stone wall. "What is this, Alphonse? Can it be a zebra?"

"Ha! *Oui!*" said Alphonse, amused by their surprise. "The empress has a whole menagerie, gifts from Napoleon's travels or homage from other explorers. The zebra is perfectly safe, but I must advise you to avoid the ostrich. The feathers are *très à la mode* on your cap, but the bird itself is a horrible creature." Alphonse shuddered. "I ran afoul of him once and he tried to bat me down like one of your English cricket players. Urgh!"

They passed more exotic animals behind the stone walls, a far different sight than the usual countryside sheep. By the time the carriages had come to stop in front of the chateau, they had glimpsed an Australian kangaroo, an Alpine chamois, and a very furious long-necked black bird whom Alphonse said was *not* the ostrich but was its smaller cousin, the emu.

Louisa wondered what Gyles made of the animals, but as they advanced through the stately park, she realised that he probably had not noticed them at all, for to the right, the meadow was dominated by a great greenhouse, the back side nestled in a stand of trees. The sloping roof and front side were open to the meadow and completely made of glass. If the sun had been shining, Louisa suspected she would have been blinded by the glistening of the glass panes. Alphonse had said the empress collected roses. Did Gyles know this building was full of his favourite flowers?

"*Bon!* Here we are." Alphonse's own enthusiasm grew as the carriage passed out of the park and into the carefully cultivated space around the chateau. "Now you shall meet the Empress Josephine, *ma cousine*." He leaned forward, took Louisa's hand from across the carriage, and brought it to his lips. "But never fear. She will be delighted with you. She loves to collect curiosities."

Louisa was not entirely sure what that meant, but she had no intention of asking Alphonse to clarify.

CHAPTER THIRTY-FOUR

Josephine

THE EMPRESS JOSEPHINE DID not greet them herself at the door, but an imposing collection of staff performed the function for her. Louisa learned from the housekeeper that Cosette would have a trundle bed in Louisa's own dressing room, Jacques would have a bed above the stables, and Gyles would be assigned a room belowstairs with other servants arriving for the house party. "When shall we meet her highness?" asked Louisa, curious as to the schedule of the house party.

"At dinner, milady," said the black-gowned domestic. She looked Louisa over appraisingly and seemed to approve of her modish carriage dress and feathered hat. "You must already be aware that her highness expects formality in dress. Her own attire sets the standard for all of Paris."

So that was how it was? Only the best for Empress Josephine. Perhaps the empress had omitted the common courtesy of greeting guests at the door so she could dazzle them more readily when she appeared in splendour on the grand staircase.

After Cosette had explored every corner of the rooms assigned to them and emptied the trunks into the wardrobes, she set about perfecting Louisa's toilette. Louisa sat silently at her dressing table, having no appetite for engaging in chatter with her lady's maid. Finally, it was time to examine the finished product.

"Does milady prefer these gowns to your English ones?"

"Yes," said Louisa, looking at her forest green dress in the cheval glass. The square necklines she had worn in London had never displayed her bosom and her height to the best advantage, but the deep curving drape of the Roman-style gown emphasised her figure. Small bronze brooches pinned the unfastened shoulders of her gown, and the white skin of her shoulders peeked through the green velvet.

"And your hair? Is it better than what your English maid could do?"

"Grasping for compliments?" said Louisa dryly. She was not in charity enough with her maid to offer them. She brushed her fingers over the soft curls of honey-gold hair that framed her face. "You do well enough. If the portraits I've seen are accurate, I shall be quite the contrast to the Empress Josephine."

"She favours white—it sorts well with her black hair, and maybe she thinks it makes her look younger. She has kept her figure quite well, even though she is old enough to be *une grand-mère*."

The empress was of an age with Mrs. Audeley? Louisa reflected that Mrs. Audeley would make a kind and understanding grandmother when Gyles finally married and had...children. She swallowed convulsively, dismayed by the picture of Gyles as a happily married country swain with a bouncing baby on his knee. His unknown wife loomed silently in the background of her imagination—no doubt, some Derbyshire miss who delighted in soil, and sunshine, and horticulture.

"And perhaps white was the colour all the women wore in Martinique," said Cosette, continuing to babble on as dressers of hair often do, "for it keeps one cool, and they say the Caribbean is warm."

"Is Empress Josephine from the New World?"

"*Oui*, she grew up there until she sailed to Paris to find a husband."

"How curious," said Louisa. She looked up at Cosette. "But it sounds as if you disapprove?"

Cosette wrinkled her nose. "I would not go to Paris, mi-lady, if I were on the lookout for a husband. The best ones are found in the countryside with their plough and yoke of oxen."

"Are they indeed?" murmured Louisa. She imbued her voice with a tone of disdain. "I would not have imagined that a fine lady's maid like you would dream of rustics."

That seemed to quiet Cosette. She finished her work with deft hands, creating a circle of curls at the crown of Louisa's head. Louisa looked at herself again in the cheval glass. No, this was not the face of a gentleman-gardener's wife.

Alphonse was waiting for Louisa in the reception room when she descended for dinner. Indeed, the whole house party was waiting there for their hostess. Would Empress Josephine continue to keep them waiting? As the dinner gong rang, a force of nature entered the room with dark hair, sparkling eyes, and an elegant figure swathed with white silk.

Louisa's first impression was of Josephine's vivacity which masked her age and made her seem much younger than she was. Her second impression was of her voice, a low enchanting sound like golden bells that promised pleasure for everyone who listened.

"Ah, Phonsie, you have returned," Empress Josephine said, approaching the Comte Dammartin and depositing a kiss on his cheek. "And this must be your cousin? Or should I say, your *wife*?" Josephine laughed, a low, soothing laugh that Louisa wanted to find disagreeable but reluctantly found enthralling. She noticed that however much the empress laughed and smiled, she never opened her mouth far enough to reveal her teeth.

"How do you find Paris, Lady Louisa, after the barbarous society of London?"

"Very civilised, your highness," said Louisa, offering a curtsy. To answer anything different would have been impossible.

"You agree, then, that London is barbarous?" Josephine's eyes fastened on Louisa with the inscrutability of the Egyptian sphinx.

"Perhaps not as barbarous as the Caribbean," said Louisa. She held her breath. It was a calculated quip that would either give offence or intrigue the empress—she hoped for the latter.

Josephine paused. "*Parbleu!* You are very bold, *mademoiselle*. But you are accurate. The Caribbean *was* barbarous, I admit it. My father owned an estate called Malmaison there, and it truly was a *bad house*. It was nothing compared to this estate that I have built for myself here in France—*my* Malmaison." She took Louisa's arm in hers. "After dinner, I will show it to you. And tomorrow, my gardens."

Riding the tide of royal good will, Louisa allowed herself to be pulled into the dining room on the arm of the empress while her cousin trailed closely behind them. The other guests arranged themselves according to precedence and followed, Louisa's only claim to the seat of honour being that she had captured the empress' interest. The Général Archambeau who had so enjoyed her company at the Paris salon took the seat on Louisa's right, and Alphonse managed to insert himself on the empress' left.

The empress kept a lavish table with game from her estate and preserves made from her own garden. Louisa's father had always had expensive tastes, but even his palate would have been satisfied by the platter of roast peacock and the lobster served in the shell.

"More punch, milady?" asked a voice over her shoulder. Louisa looked up. Over the last two months, she had become used to seeing Gyles' face at her elbow, dishing food onto her plate with a serious smile. The black-haired footman in Josephine's livery was a disappointment. *"Non, merci,"* said Louisa, placing a hand over the rim of her glass.

Josephine, who had already drunk three glasses, began to laugh. "I see my Caribbean rum is not to your liking, Lady Louisa. I find it sorts well with the lemon and the cinnamon. I can rarely go to sleep without a glass of punch before bed."

Alphonse manfully took a drink of his own glass of punch. "It is an acquired taste, your highness, but for your sake, I have acquired it."

"Of course you have," said Josephine indulgently, looking at Alphonse as if he were a pet spaniel or pug. "You always do what you can to please me. I wish I could say the same for my husbands."

"Your highness has more than one?" asked Louisa, deferentially.

"Mais oui!" Josephine looked at her in surprise. "You are too young—or too English—to know my full history. I escaped the

Caribbean and came to Paris and there I married a very dashing soldier. His name was Beauharnais. A general, like the gallant Archambeau sitting beside you."

The grey-moustached general saluted Josephine with a courtly nod from his place beside Louisa. She could see that he was sitting a little taller in his chair now after their hostess had singled him out. It was an effect that Josephine had on men.

"Beauharnais gave me my children, Eugene and Hortense, but he was not a generous man in anything else. We did not sort well together, and during *la révolution*, he had many enemies." Her dark, expressive eyes opened wide. "They sent him to Madame Guillotine."

Louisa made the appropriate sound of sympathy.

"It was a difficult time," acknowledged Josephine. "There are many things I had to do to survive. Some criticised me—"

"*Non!*" said Alphonse, tossing back a glass of the rum punch. "You were magnificent. You were the toast of Paris."

"And what would you know about that, *mon enfant?*" asked Josephine. "You were no older than my little Eugene at the time."

Alphonse made a face and reached out to take her hand. "I know you, my empress. You could not have been otherwise."

Josephine laughed. "You fresh-faced flatterer. Just like Napoleon." She turned to Louisa. "He was six years younger than me, you know, when he saw me the first time. His mother did not like it. His sister did not like it. But he was so filled with fascination for me that he would not let me be. He insisted that we marry, and how could I say no?"

"How indeed?" said Louisa. Her questions had shown merely polite interest up until now, but suddenly, she was seized with the desire to know more. "Was it a...love match?"

Josephine laughed. "Oh, he loved me in his way. He still does, despite divorcing me for his Austrian broodmare. But it is only as men are capable of love—utter devotion when they remember you and a wandering eye when they forget. While we were married, the emperor had as many lovers as I have fingers."

She lifted her small hands and flourished her ringed fingers while Alphonse made a moue of horror. "Do not gasp, Phonsie! It is the truth. And then, when he divorced me earlier this year, he gave me the most ridiculous present. A model of an Egyptian temple, half the length of this table. Faugh! I sent it back to him again. I do not want your silly antiquities. I want Malmaison, I said."

"And you have it," said Louisa. "You have the house and the estate."

"Yes," said Josephine. "That is the essential thing. You will learn this, Lady Louisa, that a husband may live or die, lovers may come or go, but to have one's own property and independence, that is the essential thing."

"Your highness is very wise," said Louisa, lifting her glass of rum punch to salute her hostess. She noted the triumphant gleam in Josephine's eye as the empress looked around the green satin walls, the rich brocade drapes, and the chequered black-and-white marble of her dining room. She had come through revolution, ruination, and royal intrigue unscathed and now had time to devote her life to all the pursuits she herself enjoyed. She was a woman who would be envied by most.

But casting a look at the deep-set eyes beneath the carefully placed curls, Louisa had a fleeting suspicion that the former empress was not as happy as she claimed to be. She was independent. She was a property-owner. But she was also...alone.

CHAPTER THIRTY-FIVE

Roses

BY THE SECOND DAY of their stay, Gyles was navigating the servants' staircases at Malmaison with more confidence and less chance of losing himself somewhere in the recesses of the chateau. After breakfast, he received a message from another footman that his mistress was looking for him. He seized an umbrella, in case it might be required, and followed the other footman's directions until he found Louisa standing by the side door that led out to the garden path. She wore half boots, a flounced walking dress in the same chocolate-violet as her eyes, and a navy-blue pelisse with a matching bonnet.

"There you are, Pebble," she said brightly. "The empress means to show me her greenhouse today, and I need you to carry my basket."

At the word greenhouse, Gyles brown eyes widened. Sir Abraham Hume had piqued his interest about Josephine's rose collection, and he had caught a glimpse of the massive greenhouse on the carriage ride through the park. Had Louisa realised how meaningful it would be to him to go inside? Is that why she had invited him? Or did she simply need him to fetch and carry for her?

"Thank you," he murmured, tucking the umbrella under his arm and taking the basket she held out to him. His hands were almost trembling with anticipation.

"You're welcome," said Louisa. "I might be able to take seeds or cuttings. But only if the empress allows it." She looked at him admonishingly as if she suspected *he* might take cuttings even if it were forbidden.

Did she remember the time when he had done so at Carlton House? At times, he had the inkling that she remembered their first encounter, and at other times, he was sure that she had forgotten it entirely.

"Are you planning to propagate your own plants?" Gyles gave her a cheeky grin that was entirely improper for a footman.

"No, but I know someone who might be." She wrinkled her nose at him, her usual veil of hauteur having disappeared for just a moment.

A warm feeling of happiness spread over Gyles. She was thinking of him. Of his interests. His desires.

"Ah, there you are Lady Louisa." Empress Josephine turned the corner of the corridor and nodded toward the French doors that led outside. Gyles had caught sight of her in the many portraits about the house that featured her, her children, and Napoleon, but he had not realised until this moment how old she was. She had dressed herself in white like a spring lamb, but she was an older leg of mutton than she pretended. "I fear we may encounter a little wet while walking to the greenhouse."

"My footman has an umbrella." Louis gave Gyles a nod of appreciation.

"*Eh bien?* That is helpful." Josephine beckoned for Gyles to follow them and opened the doors to step out into the rain.

Louisa cast an apologetic look at Gyles as his long arm held the umbrella over the two ladies. The water droplets descended on his own head, running off in rivulets down his shoulder. They began to walk, Louisa and Josephine mostly shielded by the black umbrella as Gyles managed to keep their bonnets dry.

The glass house jutted up from the meadow like the centrepiece on a banquet table. A tall stand of trees filled in the background behind it, and a winding gravel path brought them through the subdued beds of the winter garden. Louisa could tell that Empress Josephine must favour the English style of gardening, for there was more whimsy and wandering here than in the geometrically precise gardens the French typically employed.

There were two servants standing at attention at the door of the greenhouse, and one of them opened it deferentially while the other took Gyles' umbrella to set it to dry. The change in temperature inside the glass building was dramatic. As soon as he entered, Gyles felt steam begin to rise off his wet livery.

Josephine discarded her own bonnet and pelisse and handed them to one of the servants. Louisa followed suit. It must have been as warm and sticky in the greenhouse as it had been on Josephine's island home of Martinique.

The empress began to lead Louisa through the rows of potted plants, a riot of foliage and flowers that were out of season with the late January weather. Gyles followed at a respectful distance, in case anything should be required of him and so that he could view the lush garden from every angle. The basket hung from his long arm, ready to be filled as soon as he received command.

Gyles began to put his French lessons to good use as he strained to translate the words, phrases, and sentences that the ladies spoke.

"Many of the plants here come from Queensland in Australia," said the Empress.

"Just like the menagerie," remarked Louisa.

"Exactly. They travelled over on the same ship as the kangaroo. One part of the greenhouse is exclusively to hold pineapples. And then the crown of the collection is, of course, the roses."

Gyles tried to move as close as he could to the ladies he was trailing. He watched Josephine take hold of a Queensland vine and show the yellow flowers to Louisa. He could see Louisa touch it gingerly with the detached indifference of someone who had never soiled her hands in dirt. She was no gardener. But Gyles found he could not like her the less just because her interests were so dissimilar to his own. It would be the height of folly to insist that a friend, a partner—a lover—have all the same interests as oneself.

They passed a tree with dark orange fruits, smaller than apples, shinier than citrus. Gyles made out the name *persimmon* on the plaque that stood nearby. The colour was exquisite, just the sort of deep vibrance that would set off the violet in Louisa's eyes. He had never seen such a fruit before, and the plaque gave the provenance as India.

They entered the section of potted rosebushes. Gyles' eyes caught on a rare species of flower. It had far fewer petals than most English roses. He read the plaque mounted on the earthenware planter: *rosa indica*. He wished he knew more about where it came from—the East, no doubt. Beside it was a *rosa centifolia,* a flower with a hundred petals. Gyles had a similar variety in his own garden, brought over from the Netherlands.

Engrossed by the perfumed array of flowers, Gyles almost forgot his place and purpose—until he heard voices behind the stand of orange trees that separated the roses from the pinery.

"Your cousin says you are here in France for amusement," he overheard the Empress say. His lessons with Cosette were truly becoming most valuable. "But why are you really here?"

Gyles heard Louisa hesitate. She was such a wary creature, wary by nature but also made more so by the vicissitudes of her own life. What would she reveal to the empress? "My uncle is trying to arrange a marriage for me that is...distasteful. I have come to France to avoid it."

"Ah. And is your uncle your guardian?"

"*Oui,* but not for much longer."

"*C'est bon.* Will you arrange your own marriage then, here in France? Something more in line with your tastes?"

"I do not know, your highness."

"Alphonse would be a good stepping-stone to something better—if you can put up with his rattle for a few years."

"A...stepping stone?"

Gyles could hear the surprise in Louisa's voice.

"*Bien sûr,* you would not wish to be tied to him forever. He will help you gain a foothold in society. You have been admitted on sufferance now, but you are still English. A wrong word, a slip of the tongue, and the French will turn on you. But as the true Comtesse Dammartin, your place will be secure. Alphonse will serve you very well, and once he is tired of you, he will not be too strict about whom you associate with. He will never even notice if you use your time to find a second husband who suits you better."

There was a rustling of leaves in the orange tree, and Gyles held perfectly still, afraid that Louisa would come around the corner and realise his proximity. He had no wish for that—not now, when he might find a window into her carefully-veiled thoughts.

"I had not thought of marriage in such terms."

Josephine gave a lilting, musical laugh. "But how else would one think of it? You are young and beautiful now, but age comes on apace. You will not always be able to command men or inspire their devotion." The empress' tone turned bitter, and Gyles remembered that her divorce from Napoleon was still of recent date. "You are like a flower on a trellis, my dear, and the winter is coming soon. You must make the most of the time you have to climb as high as you can."

"And Alphonse is your suggestion?"

"*Mais oui.* He brought you here to receive my blessing, you know."

Gyles stiffened as he overheard that last remark. The tone of Empress Josephine was coy. He wondered what exactly her relationship with the Comte Dammartin was. The mincing fop was three decades younger than her. Had he been one of her lovers?

The English newspapers were notoriously scurrilous in their charges against Bonaparte and his bride, and Gyles supposed that not every rumour about Napoleon and Josephine was true. But no one could deny that Josephine had been a courtesan before her marriage to Napoleon, and it was also frequently reported that she had taken lovers while he was gone on the front lines of battle. Dammartin, with his loose morals, could have been one of her latest beaux.

"I shall consider your suggestion," said Louisa. Gyles could not see her, but he could imagine the inscrutable, diplomatic look on her face, and he could almost hear the voices debating inside her head. On the surface, Louisa always seemed so sure of herself, so calmly assertive. But he had seen through that calm exterior, and behind the facade was a river of emotion that could rise like the Nile.

The basket dangled, forgotten, on Gyles' arm. What were roses and what were plant cuttings when Louisa's whole life was at such a turning point? Deep in her innermost heart, he did not think she was as coldly calculating as the empress. But he had seen her consider other undesirable options, like marrying Lord Kendall to avoid Mr. Digby, and he knew that she was not the type to shirk a difficult choice if she believed it to be a necessary one.

The empress was urging her to marry Alphonse. If Louisa believed that such a step would achieve the independence she so desperately wanted, was there a chance she would take it?

Chapter Thirty-Six

Cuttings

A LITTLE BEFORE NOON, a message from the house called Josephine away from her precious garden, leaving Louisa to finish the tour at her own leisurely pace. Gyles looked around to make sure the Malmaison gardeners were otherwise occupied and then approached Louisa as an equal might. "Are you enjoying yourself?"

"A better question for you, I would think."

"As you can see, I followed your instructions not to cut any flowers without invitation." It had required a good deal of self-restraint on his part, but that self-restraint had been encouraged by his concern for Louisa and his distress over the empress' advice.

"The empress gave *me* invitation to do so before she left, so I think we are safe to proceed. Come, you must tell me which ones you want, and I will cut them for you."

Gyles' eyes brightened, but he had no intention of forgetting the overheard conversation in the excitement over rose clippings. "Over here." He nodded to a variety from India. Handing the basket to Louisa, he pulled a penknife from his pocket. "Better if I cut them...there's a bit of an art to it."

She acquiesced without comment. He knelt by the rosebush to find the place where the stem met the main branch.

"This one is unique," said Louisa perfunctorily.

He looked up at her with a wry grin. "Oh, is that so, milady? And how would you say it differs from the white rose across the path?"

"Don't tease me," said Louisa, trying to be cross but unable to hold back a smile. "Not everyone can like roses as much as you do. I was just trying to be polite."

Gyles chestnut head bent back toward the rosebush. The air in the humid greenhouse felt increasingly warm. "I hope you don't feel the need to be *too* polite to your cousin."

"What do you mean?" Her voice turned suspicious.

"I overheard the empress quizzing you about him. It sounds like he's about to make you an offer."

Louisa breathed in sharply. "You understood that?" Apparently, she had been unaware of Gyles' growing abilities to understand French and was not pleased with the opportunity that it had afforded him. "What if he does? What business is that of yours?"

"None," admitted Gyles, making a sharp diagonal cut through the woody stem. He laid the piece in the basket. "I suppose marriage to your cousin would establish your place in Paris."

"Yes."

"And I suppose your cousin is a much more attractive prospect than Solomon Digby."

"Are you *trying* to convince me to accept him?"

"No," said Gyles brusquely. The penknife almost slipped and cut his finger as he was positioning himself to cut another branch. "I think it would be most unwise of you to do so."

"Why is that, Mr. Pebble?"

Slowly, Gyles rose to his feet. It was no use telling her his vague suspicions about something havey-cavey afoot with the agent from the bank. Monsieur Dupont had made no reappearance in connection with the count. But there were other objections to the Comte Dammartin. "You're almost at your majority. It's only a few more months and then you can go back to London safely. Why throw away your independence now on a frivolous fellow who is not likely to be faithful to you?"

"Could that not be said about all men? Even the enchanting Josephine could not keep Napoleon's interest forever."

"No, it could *not* be said about all men," said Gyles firmly. He leaned toward her and placed a stem inside the basket she held. Their eyes met and he saw the hard look shielding her soul underneath. It was the brittle bulwark of someone who had been wounded too often and grown armour to protect herself against further injury. "I'm sorry that you've been led to believe as much. I wish—"

"This is none of your affair," said Louisa sharply, refusing to let him say more. "Our conversation is finished, Mr. Pebble. Gather your own roses as you may." She thrust the basket into his chest, forcing him to take the handle before it dropped to the ground. "I will be returning to the house."

Without another word, she turned and hurried down the gravel path on the floor of the greenhouse until she found her bonnet and pelisse and went out the door, taking advantage of a break in the rain to return to the manor.

CHAPTER THIRTY-SEVEN
Visitors

As Louisa entered the house from the side door, she saw more visitors for Josephine's house party arriving in the grand entrance hall. She peeked around the corner of the corridor and saw a plump French matron with an even plumper husband, a few officers with epaulettes and braid, and a tall Englishman who looked decidedly familiar.

Her breath caught.

What is he doing here? Another person to notify your uncle where you are!

"Ah, Monsieur Smythe, *enchantée*," said the empress. The lanky, blond Mr. Smythe took her small hand and kissed it.

"I say, I'm enchanted too. Charming *chat-o* you have here."

Josephine gave a musical laugh and abandoned French for English. "Oh, Monsieur Smythe, you are too droll. You must make yourself at home. I cannot believe you have come all this way just to see me."

"A duty and a pleasure," said Mr. Smythe. "And of course, I bring you greetings from our mutual friend in England."

"Ah," said Josephine, and Louisa could see a sense of understanding pass between the two of them. "We will talk later. You must be tired, Mr. Smythe. And you must get your rest this afternoon, for tonight is the masquerade ball." The empress began to signal for her footmen to proceed upstairs with Mr. Smythe's things.

Louisa paused at the edge of the corridor and waited. She had no wish to encounter Horatio Smythe in the presence of Empress Josephine. He knew too much about her flight from London.

And what if Gyles encountered him? There was a chance that the two had met in London, and Mr. Smythe might reveal his real identity as an English gentleman. In that case, what possible reason could Gyles give for his domestic pretence? With the war between England and France raging, Josephine might well assume that Louisa's fictitious footman was an English spy, and that would be to no one's benefit.

Even if you're angry with him for interfering, you must warn him to avoid Mr. Smythe. It's in your own best interest as well as his.

Louisa hurried upstairs to where Cosette was laying out her ballgown for the masquerade that night. "When Gyles comes back into the house, tell him I want to speak to him."

"*Eh bien*, I will tell *Gyles*," repeated Cosette, saying the footman's first name with a twinkle in her eye. She shook out a petticoat and laid it across the chaise longue positioned near the wardrobe.

"I mean, Monsieur Pebble," said Louisa, but it was too late to dispel any ideas from Cosette's quick mind. The maid gave a tittering laugh.

"I don't know what you're imagining," Louisa said crossly, "but there's nothing between us other than prior acquaintance. You are welcome to him. You'll soon find out, though, that he's a *preux chevalier*, not a lover."

"Why, what do you mean, milady?"

Louisa was so annoyed by their recent conversation that her words came out like a cataract. "He's perfectly polite to every woman, and he always comes to the rescue when a lady needs him. But there's no special feeling there other than Christian charity."

Cosette pursed her lips sympathetically. "And you want passion, not charity, milady?"

"Yes, I suppose I do."

"That is because you are French, deep down inside, despite your English face. And we Frenchwomen will not settle for a match without passion." Cosette turned her back and began to rummage around in the wardrobe for slippers that would match the gown and a mask that Louisa could tie over her eyes with silk strings. "Your cousin is a passionate man."

"My cousin is a fool." Louisa sat on the bed. She could not remember ever speaking so frankly to another woman. Her mother had died when she was eight, and she had never had a duenna or governess whom she trusted enough to confide in.

But why should you trust this French maid? She has given you no reason to do so, and for all you know, she may relay your secrets to Gyles Audeley.

Louisa looked at Cosette bleakly, but there was something kindly in her eye that made the words continue despite her better judgement. "The empress thinks I should marry him."

Cosette clucked sympathetically, placing the red slippers on the floor beside the dressing table's chair. She handed Louisa the loo mask. "It would secure your title."

Louisa shuddered. She held the mask up to her face. "It would secure my unhappiness. I don't suffer fools gladly. But it would only be for a short time, says the empress. He would be a stepping-stone to something else."

"*Parbleu!* The empress is very cold. How will you get rid of him when you are done with him? Poison?"

"I assume she means divorce—that I should divorce the *comte* as Napoleon divorced her. It is not so frowned upon in France as it is in England." Louisa fastened the strings behind her head to hold the mask flush to her face.

Cosette shrugged. "Perhaps with the aristocracy of the world it is no matter. But me, I should not like to marry someone today and discard him tomorrow like a stale crust of bread. Why not wait to marry until you meet someone who is worthy?"

"That seems like an impossibility." Louisa's eyes flashed beneath the velvet mask, as alive as the black jet beads that were sewn around the edges.

"Does it?" Cosette unrolled a ribbon that matched the gown and laid it on the dressing table. She would lace it through Louisa's hair later. "Are you certain, milady, that you have met no one who is constant and true and kind and courageous?"

Louisa reflected. There was certainly one man who met all those criteria.

But were those the only qualities that mattered in a husband? Everything she had learned from observing her parents and her

Uncle Nigel screamed out against settling for the simple gentleman that Cosette was describing.

"Perhaps I *have* met someone like that. But I'm afraid he's neither rich, nor titled, nor well-connected. And I can't imagine he'd wish to live in London or Paris or spend any time at society events."

Cosette wrinkled her nose. "Is that what you care about?"

Louisa hesitated. She had never really asked herself that question. She had assumed that, like her mother and her father and her uncle, she would live the life expected of a highborn noblewoman—using her impending inheritance to finance her own leisure and gaiety, flitting about from amusement to amusement, seeking diversion to distract from the missing mundanities of friends, family, and home.

You deserve to shine in the highest circles. You deserve to have all of London and Paris at your feet as the Incomparable.

But what if there was something much simpler to be had from life? A house with a garden that was not just for show. A home with a husband who was not just a stepping stone. A heart with desires so completely fulfilled that it did not need society as a distraction.

Louisa took a deep breath. Even if she was willing to settle for a simpler life, that simpler life had not been offered. It was altruism, pure and simple and unsatisfying, that had led Gyles Audeley to follow her to France. He was not in love with her any more than a philanthropist was in love with a charity ward at the workhouse. And she was suddenly aware, with astonishing clarity, that altruism was not enough for her. She wanted more than chivalry. She wanted more than courtesy. She wanted Gyles Audeley's heart—now, tomorrow, and always. And if she could not have that, what else was left but a stepping stone to title and connections and the chance to use her own fortune as she pleased?

A stepping stone should be enough for you.

But it isn't...it isn't!

Louisa looked up from her internal battle and saw that Cosette was watching her face, waiting for an answer. "It doesn't matter what I care about," she said frostily, untying the loo mask and tossing it back onto the dressing table. "I already told you—he's a *preux chevalier,* not a lover." She clapped her hands to end the conversation. "No need to summon Monsieur Pebble after all. I will give you a message for him, and you can deliver it. And then I will lie down for a while until it is time to dress for dinner. If anyone comes, tell them I'm not to be disturbed."

Louisa unbuttoned her pelisse and presented her back to Cosette to be unlaced. She would alert Gyles about the presence of Mr. Smythe. But the rest of the consternation in her breast she would conceal, as she always did. After all, dissembling was the art of polite society, and she was an Incomparable.

CHAPTER THIRTY-EIGHT
More Visitors

THE ROWS OF ROSES in the glorious greenhouse spread out before Gyles like an endless encyclopaedia of knowledge. How amazing it would be to spend a month here—a year—a decade! His penknife was in his hand, and he had an open invitation to take whatever cuttings he wished. Yet he could not escape the growing sense of unease that sat on his chest like a sack of mulch.

He approached a red rose, similar to his Sweet-Scented China Rose sitting untended at Kendall House, but this one was a far deeper red. Red as sunset. Red as heart's blood.

The empress had advised Louisa to ally herself with the Comte Dammartin. And Louisa, unmoored as she was, might drift in that direction. If only he knew how to stop her from listing into the reefs. If only he knew how to drop an anchor to keep her safe in open water. The obvious solution, of course, was that she needed a better offer of marriage to keep her clear of Dammartin's proposal. But where could that be found?

With a flick of the hand, Gyles cut several dark red roses from their stem. He took a deep breath. Could *he* be that anchor. Could he, Gyles Audeley of Derbyshire, make Louisa Lymington an offer?

By temperament, Gyle could be considered a dreamer, but he was also a gardener. When one's actions are circumscribed by sun, rain, soil, and acreage, the facts of reality cannot be ignored. And right now, the facts were these: Louisa was the daughter of a duke. Her father had consorted with the heir to the English throne. Her mother had frequented Versailles and dined with Marie Antoinette. What would a woman like that ever see in a country gentleman like Gyles Audeley?

And yet, Gyles also knew enough about Louisa to see that, beneath all her scorn and self-possession, she was as tender and vulnerable as a wounded dove. He knew that even though her heart was bruised, it still beat true and kind and strong.

She valued fidelity. She longed for companionship. She dreamed of love. Would she trust him enough to believe that he could give it to her? Would she trust him enough to turn her back on everything else?

Gritting his teeth, Gyles tossed the deep red roses into the basket and put the penknife away. He strode toward the door of the greenhouse and took up the umbrella he had left with the empress' servant. He knew he was leaving behind the greatest treasure trove of rosarian knowledge in the world. But there was no time for that now. He would have decades of time to scribble notes about flowers, but as the poet advised, he had other rosebuds to gather today.

The rain had stopped, and Gyles stabbed the tip of the umbrella into the gravel walkway repeatedly as he hurried back to the house with long strides. He did not see any of the other guests out taking the air in the gardens—no doubt they were enjoying the warm fireplaces and more of the Empress Josephine's punch—but as he neared the house, he heard muffled voices filtering through the leaves of a tall, manicured hedge.

The substantial boxwood separated the main garden from the house, and the word *Warrenton* spoken with a French accent wafted through the damp air. Gyles halted in his tracks. Who was there and what were they talking about? The Duke of Warrenton? He moved closer to the hedge and listened intently.

It did not take long to realise that one of the voices, the excitable one, belonged to the Comte Dammartin. The other voice took a little longer for Gyles to place, but when the word *vendre* surfaced, he knew the man immediately. It was Monsieur Dupont from the bank. Why the blazes had he travelled all the way to Malmaison from Paris? Surely, *he* had not been invited as a guest?

This conversation was a little more difficult to make out than the one between the Empress and Louisa, but as he listened, bits and pieces began to come together like a schoolboy's paper puzzle.

"...our agent came back from England...it's all confirmed. She's rich. An heiress, just like she claimed to be."

"And the uncle?"

"...nowhere to be found...she's all alone."

The comte began to laugh, a less pleasant laugh than Gyles had heard him use before. "I don't suppose there's anyone to object then if I marry her *immédiatement*."

"It would certainly help your financial difficulties."

"...how soon...draw on her funds?"

"*La Banque de France* will extend you credit until arrangements can be made."

"...very well then...opportunity tonight. The Empress is holding a grand ball...."

As Gyles listened, his hand gripped the umbrella handle like a truncheon, and the wicker basket was in danger of deconstructing beneath his grip. It was good that he had no skill with pistols, for if he had, he would have been tempted to call the Comte Dammartin out for his mercenary machinations.

The voices began to grow louder, and Gyles could tell they were moving in his direction. He walked as quietly as he could along the gravel path and then made a dash for the side entrance of the house. Success! He closed the door behind him and began to walk at a more sedate pace through the halls.

The anger in his own breast surprised him. He had been angry before, at mildew, at blight, at laziness and at bad management. At poor manners, at insolence, at injustice, and at cruelty. But this was something different. This time it was anger mixed with passion building to a maelstrom inside his chest. How dare the count think that Louisa was weak and worthless enough to be gammoned in such a manner? How dare he treat her like a disposable doll without a mind, a heart, or dreams of her own? He was just like her father, just like her uncle, just like the odious Mr. Digby.

Emotions churning, Gyles advanced down the corridor bristling like an untamed beast from the Empress' Australian menagerie. "There you are!" said a feminine voice in his native English. Gyles halted in annoyance as Cosette removed the umbrella from his grip, seized his sleeve, and pulled him towards the servants' staircase.

"Where are you taking me?" he demanded, the wicker basket with the rose cuttings jostling against the brass buttons of his livery. "I need to speak with Lady Louisa."

"I can assure you," said Cosette, refusing to loosen her grip, "that she has no interest in speaking with you right now. But she bade me deliver you a message, about a certain Englishman that she thinks it best you avoid." She dragged him into the servants' staircase and shut the door.

Exasperated, Gyles pulled the uncomfortable wig from his head and threw it into the basket with the flowers. He raked a hand through his tangled chestnut hair. His impatient voice rose to a louder pitch than usual. "I don't care whether it interests her. She needs to know what I have to tell her."

"Monsieur Pebble," said Cosette sternly, "surely a message from your mistress must take precedence over your own. Lady Louisa says she wants you to avoid Mr. Horatio Smythe."

"And I want *her* to avoid that slimy cad the Comte Dammartin," boomed Gyles. A housemaid using the servants' staircase skittered past them like a cautious mouse, sending Gyles a confused look over her shoulder. The girl was doubtless unused to a foreign tongue being spoken in a back stairwell with such vehemence and ferocity.

The pair maintained an awkward silence until the housemaid disappeared. Then Cosette began to laugh, a giddy, happy laugh that filled the whole staircase. "Oh, Monsieur Pebble, I was afraid that you would be too shy like a kitten, but I see now you are a lion at heart. *Bravo, monsieur.* You will *make* her listen to you."

Confused by this sudden approbation, Gyles pulled away from Cosette and started up the stairs.

"*Mais non!*" interjected Cosette. "You cannot see her now." Once again, she reached up and laid a hand on his sleeve, arresting his motion as he stood on the winding steps above her. "She is resting her eyes. A sleeping beauty, *n'est-ce pas?* Her prince must wait."

Gyles fervently hoped that the prince she referred to was himself and not the Comte Dammartin. He gritted his teeth. "But there is something I must tell her. The sooner the better."

Cosette placed her hands on her hips. "You've waited this long to speak—surely, you can wait a little longer. When she wakes, she will be busy preparing for the masquerade ball. I intend to make her my masterpiece, and you will not disturb her at her toilette."

Gyles' chin lifted. The masquerade ball? Surely that was the opportunity Alphonse had mentioned. He could not wait till tomorrow to warn her about her cousin's jaded intentions. A secluded upbringing in the English countryside had never afforded Gyles the opportunity to attend a masquerade ball. But it did not take much of an imagination to suppose what freedom of address might be employed when every man's identity was hidden by a mask. He had a presentiment that Alphonse was intending to use the event to press his own suit. He needed to give Louisa a warning—and an alternative—before that foppish fortune hunter wore down her defences. "How many people will be at the ball?"

Cosette shrugged. "Seventy-five? A hundred? The other maids say that the empress has invited the surrounding gentry as well as her house guests."

"And all the guests will be in evening dress and masks?"

"Of course. It is a masquerade."

"*Très bien*," he said, his accent still pronounced but becoming less noticeable. "I have a set of evening wear in my satchel. If you were to repair the wrinkles and find me a mask, I could blend in with the crowd and find a chance to speak with Lady Louisa."

Cosette gasped in mock horror. "A footman at the Empress' masquerade?"

Gyles paused. He gripped the handle of the staircase. "Cosette, I have a confession to make. I'm not exactly a footm—"

"*Parbleu!*" said Cosette, before he could finish his statement. "You think I do not know that? You think I cannot tell a beeswax candle from a tallow one? Of course, you are a gentleman, and not a footman." She gave a girlish giggle. "I can tell you now that Jacques and I have a wager—to which one of us will you admit it first? I cannot wait to see him and tell him that I have won the prize."

The ridiculousness of the situation struck Gyles, even as the anxiety of his need to see Louisa still weighed on his breast. "So, you've seen through my poor disguise all along? What gave it away? My ineptitude at dinner service? Or my inability to answer the door promptly?"

"More likely the sheep's eyes you made at milady whenever she came in the room."

"Hmm," said Gyles. "The more fool me. I'm glad you've won the wager. Will you also help me win my lady?"

"*Mais oui!*" said Cosette, exploding into a ball of furious energy. "Send me your evening wear, and the wrinkles, they shall be gone within the hour. And a mask, I will find you one. And a domino as well." Cosette looked at him in glee. "Oh, Monsieur Pebble, I was afraid that you did not have what it takes to woo a Frenchwoman, but I think you will do. You will do very nicely." She darted up three stairs and, standing on tiptoe, placed a friendly kiss on his cheek. "*Une bouche* from Cosette Bouchard. For luck, Monsieur Pebble." She gave a squeak of delight and clapped her hands together.

CHAPTER THIRTY-NINE
Masquerade

Louisa was not looking forward to this masquerade. Long ago, at the tender age of seven, she had observed a masquerade through the spindles of the upstairs bannister at her London home. It had been a raucous affair full of provocative colour and bawdy braggadocio. She remembered seeing her mother dressed as a voluptuous Bo Peep with huge panniers and curved shepherd's crook, neither of which served to keep a flock of gentlemen admirers at bay. She remembered seeing her father dressed as a Methodist clergyman, but not the sort of clergyman who should be left alone with the female members of his flock.

As a debutante last year, such events had been off-limits. Louisa's many conquests had been achieved at more insipid events like Almack's and afternoon tea. But Paris had a more liberal view of propriety for unmarried women. The masquerade was *de rigeur* for Josephine's houseguests, and more than a few extra visitors had driven out to Malmaison that afternoon to enjoy the sumptuous occasion.

"Will you wear the sapphires?" Cosette asked, as she put the finishing touches on Louisa's honey-coloured curls. Louisa looked down at her fiery gown, a deep, deep orange with red embroidery about the neck and hem. It was the colour of the persimmons in Malmaison's greenhouse with a touch of fire along the edges.

"Rubies would be more fitting."

"Why not roses?" said Cosette. She reached for the basket that Louisa had abandoned earlier in the greenhouse, a basket that had mysteriously made its way upstairs although its bearer had not shown his face in the last several hours. Inside were several stems of deep red roses.

"Roses," repeated Louisa.

Surely not. You cannot wear roses. You know who cut those stems.

Louisa picked up a flower from the basket—a red so dark and deep it looked like rubies still embedded in the ground. A thorn on the stem caught her finger, and the sharp stab of pain soon gave way to a drop of blood. It was not the first time a thorn had pricked her hand. Her mind flew back to Carlton House so many years ago, and the face of Gyles Audeley trespassed once again in the garden of her heart.

"Very well," said Louisa, in a moment of weakness. "I will wear the roses in my hair."

"And in your bosom?" asked Cosette, irrepressible as always.

"In my *hair*, Cosette," said Louisa with a flash of hauteur. Her gown was cut low enough as it was—she did not need a flower to draw attention to her decolletage.

By the time Cosette had pinned the roses in Louisa's curls, it was nearly time to go downstairs. Louisa fastened the jet-studded loo mask over her eyes, aware that it would fool none of the fellow guests with whom she had already dined. It might be enough to shield her identity from Mr. Smythe, however, if he was unaware she was in residence. She had no desire for Horatio Smythe to reminisce about the time he had spotted the runaway heiress in a hackney leaving Grosvenor Square in the dead of night.

For the evening's entertainment, the music room at Malmaison had been converted into a ballroom, with the salon next to it dedicated to those who would rather play cards than dance. The dance floor could fit thirty couples comfortably, and when Louisa descended the stairs, she discovered that the music had already begun. A whiskered harlequin in a mask took her hand and kissed it. "*Enchanté, mademoiselle.*" It was a strangely undignified costume in which to find the Général Archambeau. He reserved a dance on her card and was followed in swift succession by a Hussar, a Roman centurion, and a knight.

The next to approach was an Arabian prince, whom Louisa immediately identified as Alphonse. His average height was augmented by a towering turban, and a coloured ostrich plume bobbed and swayed above him with each mincing step. "Ah, *ma cherie,* you are looking divine. I hope you have saved the supper dance for me." He refused to let go of her gloved hand until she withdrew it with greater force than was polite, and there was an amorous—or was it acquisitive?—glitter in his eye.

Louisa looked down at her card. Unfortunately, yes, the supper dance was still free. She reluctantly pencilled in Alphonse's name. At least he would be constrained by the public nature of supper to keep his hands to himself.

"No jewels tonight?" he said, his eyes lowering to her neck.

"I chose roses instead," said Louisa simply. She clutched a handful of her fiery skirt so her slippered feet could move more quickly to another corner of the room.

It was almost time to take the floor with Général Archambeau when an unknown man materialised behind her shoulder. He was several inches taller than her, and atop his eveningwear, he wore only a black mask and a simple black domino with a hood. "Does milady have any dances left?" It was clear from his accent that his French was not fluent. Without turning her head to face him fully, Louisa could not tell if she had met him before. The tone of voice, however, had a familiar ring to it. Could it be Mr. Smythe? He was tall and English. She had never heard him speak French, but it was not hard to imagine that he did not do it well.

"I have one more dance after supper," said Louisa. She offered him her card and pencil. He took it and scrawled a name. But before she could read it, her harlequin arrived to carry her off into the swirling dance.

The supper dance, which Louisa was dreading, came even sooner than she expected. Her Arabian prince, whom she had never before seen without an elaborate cravat and padded shoulders, had taken his costume quite seriously. A purple embroidered vest hung open over his linen shirt, with a neckline even more plunging than her own, reaching all the way down to his wide embroidered sash. His Arabian trousers gathered around the ankle, revealing embroidered slippers with pointed toes that matched the purple of the rest of his costume.

"I see you are admiring my costume," said Alphonse smugly. Beneath the cutouts of his mask, his eyes were lined with kohl. Louisa could not imagine any English gentleman of her acquaintance adopting such a style.

"I believe it is more generally accepted for the gentleman to admire the lady," said Louisa tartly.

"*Mais certainement!*" Alphonse squeezed her hand as he led her into the next figure of the dance. "It goes without saying that you are exquisite. A little taller than is desirable, but I do not think anyone will comment on that."

"No, no one but you," murmured Louisa. The turban with the bobbing ostrich feather was assuredly a sop to his vanity so that he did not feel short in her presence.

"You spent the morning with the empress in her garden. I wonder, did she share my secret with you?"

Louisa's eyes widened with annoyance. She was glad that the next dance figure took her to another partner before she had time to answer Alphonse. When they came back together, her face was perfectly composed. "Surely a gentleman does not inquire what ladies speak of in private?"

"But a cousin may inquire, may he not?" Alphonse executed the next allemande with a flourish. "*Eh bien,* perhaps we can find a private moment ourselves, and I will whisper my secret in your beautiful ear."

"And miss our supper? Surely not."

Alphonse's nostrils flared. "After supper then. Let us go out to the garden together."

"But the roses will make you sneeze," said Louisa with mock sympathy. "I could not think of torturing you so."

The dance ended, and Louisa continued to manage Alphonse all through supper. They sat far enough away from the head of the table that they could not speak with Josephine, but Louisa could see their hostess sitting several chairs away, displaying a coy smile that came from her hazel eyes and showed none of her teeth. Louisa eyed the skilful maquillage and careful tailoring that kept Josephine as flawlessly fresh as a woman half her age. Louisa had submitted herself to Cosette's careful ministrations for over an hour. She shuddered to think how long Josephine would have to sit at her toilette each day.

Beside the empress was a slender, fair-haired fellow with a swan mask. Louisa recognized him right away as Horatio Smythe. His mannerisms were too noticeable for it to be otherwise. But if Mr. Smythe was a swan, then who was the fellow in the black domino who had claimed the next dance with her? Try as she could, Louisa could not see him anywhere at the long dining table. She remembered her dance card, tied to her wrist with a small piece of string. Unfolding it, she looked for the name written after the supper dance.

"Are you listening to me, *cherie?*" asked Alphonse, who was continuing to babble on about his need to share a certain secret with her.

Louisa stared at him blankly. No, she was not. For the name written on her card for the next dance was none other than *Monsieur Pebble.*

CHAPTER FORTY

Heart's Blood

GYLES HUNG BACK IN the anteroom all through dinner, but when the guests returned to the ballroom, he was immediately at Louisa's shoulder. Earlier, when he had asked for the dance, she had been unsure of his identity, but he could tell, by the lift of her chin, that she knew him now.

"I was not aware you were invited to this masquerade, Monsieur Pebble."

"That's the delightful thing about masks—invitations can't always be verified." He held out his hand.

She hesitated for a moment and then placed her gloved hand in his.

Gyles might not have been a consummate cosmopolitan, but his mother's tutelage had ensured that he was a competent dancer. They danced in silence. But even though there were no words between them, each reconnection of their fingers and interlacement of their arms became more and more charged like a lowering sky before a coming lightning storm. Gyles' blood began to pulse, both with the exertion of moving through the room and the excitement of feeling Louisa's fingertips against his arm and palm.

The lady herself was not immune to the sensations. The longer the dance went on, the higher her colour rose. Finally, it seemed that she could stand it no more. She stepped out of the set and began to fan herself with her hand. "Mr. Pebble, I am overheated. Perhaps we might go outside to get some air."

Gyles offered her his arm. They exited the music room, passed through the adjoining salon, and found a stair leading outside. "It is freezing out there," said Gyles. "Milady will be cold."

"I don't care," said Louisa, walking abruptly to the opening and pushing her way into the dark chill. Gyles set his lips into a firm line and then followed her, removing the hooded domino as he walked. "Here." He pulled it gently over her head, the billowing garment covering her exposed shoulders and neckline. A rose caught on it and, coming unpinned from her curls, fell to the ground. She accepted the domino without comment and kept walking.

Gyles bent down to pick up the fallen rose—the favour that he had given to her and that she had chosen to wear. He gripped it tightly between thumb and forefinger and followed her down the path. Where was she going? Those silken dance slippers would not get far on outdoor terrain.

Gyles looked past her and saw the lights of the glass house ahead. Heated even at night, it would be a refuge from the January air. Louisa hurried ahead of him along the gravel path, blending in with the night in the hooded domino and the jet-studded loo mask.

A servant opened the door of the greenhouse for Louisa and left it ajar for Gyles who was not far behind. Apparently,

Josephine and her guests were used to visiting the greenhouse at all hours. The eerie glow of a few scattered torches and heating braziers illuminated the building. Louisa walked until she came to the very rosebush that Gyles had plundered earlier that day. Red as sunset. Red as rubies. Red as heart's blood.

Louisa turned around to face her pursuer. Beneath her mask, Gyles saw her violet eyes, illuminated by the distant torches and glowing with luminous intensity. "Why are you here, Gyles?"

He pulled off the mask that covered the top half of his face and tossed it on the ground. "I came to warn you about your cousin."

"You already did that this morning."

"Yes, but now I have proof that he is filled with ill-intent. I overheard him meeting with Monsieur Dupont from your bank. He has been investigating your finances, with an eye to marrying a rich bride."

"He needs the money?"

"He's bankrupt. Apparently, the title Napoleon gave him did not come with much of a stipend."

Louisa began to laugh. "You act as if I should be shocked. My fortune has been a prime consideration for every man who's ever looked at me. I would be more shocked if the Comte Dammartin did *not* want my money. Why else would he pursue me?"

Gyles stared at her, dismayed by her dismissal of her own worth. Her fortune was nothing compared with herself. He took a step closer.

"Why are *you* here, Gyles?" Her voice, so cuttingly sardonic a moment before, took on a tone of confusion as he continued to approach.

"Because where you are, there I must be too, to serve you in whatever capacity I can."

Her flawless face crinkled into a frown. "Because you are a collector of kind deeds, of chivalrous gestures, and hospitable endeavours." Her voice was bitter now. He could almost smell the salt water imprisoned at the back of her throat.

"No." He was close enough to touch her now, but he refrained from reaching out. "Because I cannot bear to be separated from you." He held out the rose that had fallen from her hair. "Heart's blood, Louisa. That's what I call this one. And heart's blood is what you are to me."

Slowly, Louisa reached out her hand to take the flower, but rather than letting go, Gyles enveloped her fingers in his own. Her gloved hand did not pull back, and slowly, ever so slowly, his calloused thumb began to trace a path across her knuckles.

"Take off your mask, Louisa. Please." He held his breath, trying to keep from alarming her, hoping that she would understand the meaning of his words.

She raised her left hand and pulled back the hood of the domino. For a few seconds, her fingers struggled with the strings tied behind her curls. "I can't do it on my own," she said at last. "It's too tight."

He pressed the rose into her right hand and then released it. "Let me help." Lifting his hands to the nape of her neck, he began to loosen the knotted string buried in her honey-gold curls. His wrists flanked the sides of her neck, and their pulses began to beat in unison.

After a moment's effort, the black mask, studded with jet beads, fluttered forlornly to the ground.

"Why are you here, Gyles?" breathed Louisa, for the third time.

"For this," said Gyles. He leaned in and pressed his lips against hers.

CHAPTER FORTY-ONE

Flight

LOUISA HAD WITNESSED MANY kisses in life and in art that had made the activity seem tawdry or even lascivious. She had repulsed a few such kisses from men like the Earl of Yarmouth that had filled her with disgust and chagrin. But this kiss had nothing crude about it. Respectfully, determinedly, Gyles' lips met her own with a firm pressure that began to shift and grow and burn as the swirling heat of the greenhouse enveloped them both. His arms came around her like cradling vines. Her own hands lifted involuntarily, like sunflowers to the warmth of the sun, until they caressed his face and buried themselves in his chestnut hair.

Gyles gave a sigh and deepened the kiss, and Louisa responded in kind. Never had she thought that a kiss could be like this—a joining of herself, body and soul, to one who truly cared about her, and her alone. Never had she thought that an embrace could be so pure—the tender caresses of a man who found her infinitely more meaningful than a beautiful face or a bountiful fortune.

But how do you know that? Parents, uncle, suitors, servants—they've all abandoned you before. How can you ever believe that another person truly cares for you more than they care for their own interests?

Bewildered by the questions that raced through her mind, she began to pull away.

"Louisa," said Gyles, his voice a low growl. His muscled arms refused to let her go, and she felt him drawing her closer into the circle of his quiet strength. "Stop thinking. Tell that voice in your head to be quiet."

"But what if that voice is true?" she whispered.

"It isn't," said Gyles with the calm assurance of a man who could dig in the rockiest soil and still bring forth beauty. "If it tells you I don't love you, then it's a liar and a cheat. If it tells you that I'll ever leave you, then it's as false as Spanish coin."

"You love me?" Her heart flipped over inside her chest.

"I wouldn't have traipsed across the Channel in a scratchy wig and toe-murdering shoes for any other reason."

"Gyles!" she protested but got no further, for the kiss her doubts had interrupted had begun again in earnest.

Later, after they had found a bench, and shared more confidences, and kissed again, Louisa's practical self began to surface. "What now, Gyles? What do we do? I'm afraid Alphonse might make Paris too hot to hold us once he finds out I won't have him. And Empress Josephine too—she wanted us to make a match of it. She still has Napoleon's ear, and I have no official papers allowing me to stay. We could end up locked away in some old Bourbon prison, or worse."

"Then let's leave France. Tonight. Without any fanfare or farewell."

"Where would we go?"

"I may not have a grand mansion like Malmaison, but I live quite comfortably in Derbyshire. My mother can chaperone us until the banns are read."

"I won't be able to marry you without my uncle's permission until I come of age in April."

"Then I'll be your footman for a few more months, but I can't promise I won't steal a kiss while I'm serving you dinner."

"Oh Gyles," said Louisa reprovingly, lured by the mention of such a thing into stealing her own kiss at that very moment. "Mmm. Then it's decided. I'll have Cosette pack my things. Tell Jacques that we leave Malmaison tonight."

"Yes, milady," said Gyles with a grin, pulling his forelock as a proper footman would. He stood up from the bench and helped her to her feet.

"I'm afraid I must get used to no longer ordering you about," she said with chagrin.

"I don't think that's a habit you will ever break," teased Gyles. He took her hand and kissed it. "But as long as you punctuate your commands with a kiss, I'll take them under consideration."

***

It was fortunate that Louisa had brought her own carriage and driver to Malmaison and, thus, was not dependent on Alphonse for means to depart. In the room above the stables, Jacques Martin was snoring loudly when Gyles rousted him from his bed. He sputtered awake as Gyles gave him a firm nudge.

"Harness the horses," murmured Gyles. "And do it quietly. We don't want to attract attention."

Jacques grunted in response and followed Gyles down the stairs as soon as he found his coat and breeches. For such a large man, he was surprisingly light on his feet and deft with his hands. Gyles heard barely a jingle of the harness as the driver coaxed the first horse into the carriage traces. But right as Jacques led the second horse out of its stall, a loud squawk filled the air. The horses began to stamp nervously until Jacques soothed them with a hand on each of their foreheads.

"What was that?" whispered Gyles. "Surely not a stallion?"

Jacques began to laugh softly. "A demon, Monsieur Pebble."

There was no time to elucidate that mystery. Gyles left Jacques to his work and returned to the house to change his clothing. It would preserve Louisa's reputation far better if he could continue to travel in the guise of a footman. And if he could avoid making sheep's eyes at Louisa—as Cosette had claimed he did—then no one would know that his brass-buttoned livery hid a heart that was wholly in thrall to its mistress.

He no longer had a mask to shield his face, so he spent some time skirting the busy servants who might recognize him. Eventually, he was able to slip undetected belowstairs as strains of music were still pouring from the ballroom. Once he had discarded his eveningwear and changed back into the garb of a footman, he mounted the stairs to the second floor to see how Louisa was getting on.

"*Eh bien!* There you are, Monsieur Pebble," said Cosette, peeking her head out from the bedroom door as if she had been waiting for him. "She says she will bring nothing, that she already has everything she needs." Cosette arched a disapproving eyebrow.

"And what do you say?"

"That if she becomes seasick on the packet to England, she will want another dress to wear! A woman needs more than love, I say. She needs a fresh shift and an extra walking dress."

Gyles poked his head into the bedroom and saw that Louisa had already changed into a more serviceable gown—a dark blue carriage dress that would draw far less attention than her fiery ballgown—and a pair of half boots. "Pack just the smallest trunk," he said, "for you and Cosette, and I will carry it down after you are safely outside."

"Ah, you are giving *me* orders now I see." It was the sort of thing the Louisa of two months ago might have said, but her eyes had such an expression of tenderness, that Gyles could see she took no affront.

"Hurry, darling," he urged, and stepped back into the corridor to keep watch. From the open door, he heard Cosette gasp and giggle, *"Oh la la!"*

Let her giggle—her meddling had been invaluable in bringing him together with Louisa, and for that he was grateful.

Within minutes, Louisa and Cosette exited the room, both wearing dark cloaks over their travelling dresses. Gyles nodded to them that the corridor was all clear, and they hurried down the stairs. The newly packed trunk lay just inside the door. Gyles hefted it onto his shoulder and peered out into the corridor again. A pair of footmen were striding down the hall. He closed the door and waited. Whereas Louisa and Cosette might plead a nocturnal walk in the gardens if they were questioned, the trunk he bore on his shoulders was an unmistakable sign of flight. Two minutes later, he cracked the door open an inch. The corridor was empty.

With the guests engaged in the ballroom, he decided that the main staircase was safer than the servants' stair. He went downstairs and out the doors that led to the path. The way to the stables veered off in the other direction from the gardens. With the great glass house behind him, he hurried through the dark and cold back to the stables where the others were waiting.

CHAPTER FORTY-TWO

Confrontation

G YLES HAD NOT YET reached the stables when a faint feminine shriek pierced the dark air. Deuce take it! Was that Louisa? Cosette? Gyles increased his pace, trying to run as the unwieldy trunk bumped and bruised his straining shoulder. A great thud followed by a clatter met his ears. From inside the stable walls, he heard a lifted voice that was incontrovertibly Louisa's. "Stop it! You must not hurt him."

Gyles skidded to a halt, stepped off the path, and laid the trunk on the ground. The "him" must refer to Jacques, and if that mountain of a man had been harmed by someone, it was best to proceed cautiously. There was a small door at the side of the stable that opened to a workroom. Hanging on the shadowy wall were pitchforks, shovels, brooms, and other implements for scouring the stables. Gyles took down a shovel and peeked through the leather flap that separated the workroom from the main stables.

The lit carriage lanterns showed Jacques pinned to the floor with a footman muscling down each of his arms and another sitting on his legs. They were all wearing the Empress Josephine's livery, but it was no mystery whose orders they were obeying. "Hold him down!" shouted Alphonse, distracted with trying to do the same to Louisa. She was almost a match for him, and he had much ado to keep her from clawing his face. Cosette was nowhere to be seen. Jacques let out a groan and closed his eyes. They must have surprised him with a hit to the head before knocking him down onto the hay, but they were wise enough not to release his arms and legs, for if he made it back onto his feet, he could easily have cracked their skulls together.

Gyles grimaced. Now would have been a good time to be a master of the fencing sabre, or at least, a decent shot with a brace of pistols in his hands. But as fate would have it, he was not a dashing Corinthian, but only a gentleman-gardener from Derbyshire. And the only weapon in his possession was a long-handled shovel used for scraping up manure.

Louisa gave another scream and Gyles, from behind the leather flap, could see that Alphonse had twisted her arms behind her back without any consideration for the pain it would cause. *"C'est incroyable!"* he bellowed. "That you would try to leave without at least a good-bye, after all that I have done for you. I gave up Hortense. And Mireille as well. I would have bestowed on you the name you tried to steal. But how do you repay me? With scorn! With contempt! You prefer your footman as a lover."

Louisa tried to stomp on Alphonse's foot with her half boot, but he saw what she was about and avoided the blow. Manhandling her roughly, he used one arm to hold her hands behind her and pulled her against his open-necked shirt with the other.

His tall turban with the outrageous ostrich feather bobbed in the carriage light as he declared his displeasure.

"But what you do not count on is that Josephine is my friend. She knows everything that occurs at Malmaison. She has ears at every door and eyes at every window. She tells me her servants have observed your greenhouse tryst. She tells me you have changed into travelling clothes and left with your maid through the front door."

He pulled her closer so that his mouth was directly beside her ear. "*Eh bien,* you'll not make a fool of Alphonse in such a way. If you won't marry me by fair means, I'll have you by foul ones. I'll—"

A thud sounded, stopping Alphonse's impassioned threats. Gyles had slipped behind him in the shadows and delivered a mighty blow to the back of his head with the metal shovel. As Alphonse reeled and staggered, Gyles reached for Louisa and pulled her behind him. The footmen began to jabber at each other in consternation, but he could see that they dared not let go of Jacques in case the huge Samson regained his strength.

Unfortunately, the Arabian prince's turban had taken a great deal of the shovel's force. Instead of falling to the ground, Alphonse righted himself within a few seconds and pulled a pistol out of the purple sash wrapped around his middle. It was the sort of small pistol a lady might carry in her muff, or a country doctor might carry in his pocket. But it was still deadly enough to kill and Alphonse was demented enough to fire it.

"At last! The footman shows his face." He raised the barrel of the gun. Louisa wriggled out of Gyles' protective grasp and stepped in front of him.

"Out of the way, *ma cousine,*" shrilled Alphonse. "When we are married, you may have your *amours* with the proper class, but I draw the line at servants."

"You do?" called a sunny voice from the darkened stalls at the far end of the stable. It was Cosette, closer than anyone had expected, and foolishly giving away her own position in order to make a point. "That wasn't apparent when you offered to make me your mistress after you'd married my lady."

Alphonse let out a cry of annoyance along with a string of French words that Cosette had omitted to teach Gyles. The pistol began to wave erratically in his hand.

As Gyles attempted to pull Louisa back out of harm's way, he heard the rasping noise of a metal bolt being drawn. One of the stalls was opening. He could only assume that Cosette had done it. A cascade of strange, clattering foot beats reverberated across the floorboards of the stable. No horse's hooves had ever made that sound. What strange beast had fearless Cosette unleashed into their midst?

A horrendous squawk filled the air. Jacques' horses began to whinny and shuffle in terror, pushing the carriage back against the water trough. Was this the demon that Jacques had mentioned earlier?

Josephine's footmen, clearly cognizant of what was about to befall, leaped up from their post and fled as fast as their stockinged legs could take them, out of the stable and into the night. Jacques lifted himself onto his hands and knees and crawled weakly over to the carriage, trying to calm the horses with clucks and hums. Meanwhile, Gyles propelled Louisa backwards towards the wall. Just as the shrieking ostrich reached them, they ducked beneath the leather flap that led to the workroom full of tools.

Alphonse, alone in the path of the bird's fury, let out a scream shriller than that of the ostrich. The gun fired into the air. But the Frenchman, it seemed, was even a worse shot than Gyles, and the bullet embedded itself into the wall of the stable. Attracted by the sound of Alphonse's screaming—or perhaps by the bobbing plume atop his turban—the long-legged bird ran at the count with outstretched neck.

It was not the French aristocracy's finest moment. Wailing with fear, Alphonse tore his turban from his head, tossed it at the snapping beak, and then took to his heels as fast as his pointed slippers would carry him. The ostrich followed, shrieking like an archfiend. As Gyles and Louisa held each other tightly in the stable workroom, they could hear the screams of the fleeing victim as the demon of Malmaison chased him into the night.

CHAPTER FORTY-THREE
Homeward

As Alphonse disappeared from the scene, Louisa let out a sigh of relief. She felt herself go limp against Gyles firm chest. His hands came around her waist to hold her up, a gesture far more intimate than the slight support he had rendered so long ago in Hatchard's bookstore.

"Well, Julia, was my interruption superfluous this time?"

Julia...? Julia!

As Louisa heard him say that name, half of the air left her body. All this time, when she thought he had forgotten, that memory of Carlton House had always been there. He had remembered their first meeting. He had remembered *her*.

"Have you always known it was me?" she demanded.

"Of course," said Gyles, lifting a hand to caress her cheek. "From the moment I saw you in the hallway at Kendall House. *There she is*, I thought, *the most beautiful flower in the Carlton House garden*."

"Well, you certainly didn't show it. I thought you were as oblivious as an Oxford professor."

"You were obviously pretending to be someone else. I didn't want to give it away before Mr. Digby did."

Louisa leaned into the hand that lay against her cheek. "Thank you. For the interruption in the pavilion. And for the interruption today."

He gave her a lopsided grin. "I may not know how to shoot or fence, but I *can* handle myself with a shovel."

"And you're quite adept at rescuing ungrateful damsels from perilous predicaments."

"Oh, this one will be grateful," said Gyles. "I'm sure of it." His face descended towards hers in the dark, and his nose nuzzled her cheek as his lips searched for hers.

"I love you, Gyles," said Louisa, filled with a desperate urgency to say those words aloud, words that she had never uttered in the whole of her life. Not to her mother, not to her father, not to a single soul in all of England or France.

"I was hoping you might," said Gyles. "And that's quite fortuitous, for I love you too." His lips found hers in the darkness, and they held onto each other with an even greater understanding and confidence than they had enjoyed in the glass greenhouse one short hour ago.

⁂

"Shouldn't we be going?" interrupted Cosette, peeling back the leather flap that covered the entrance to the workroom.

"Erm, yes, of course," said Gyles, reluctantly separating from Louisa. It was painful to pull away from her after they had finally come to such an understanding, but there would be other opportunities for affection and time was of the essence.

As they emerged into the main stable, hand in hand, Gyles saw that Jacques had soothed the horses until they were able to stand composedly. The large man was holding a handkerchief to the contusion at the back of his head, a petite, lace-trimmed handkerchief that he must have obtained from Cosette.

"They waylaid me before I knew they were coming," he grumbled, gesturing to a stout pole lying on the hay that the Empress' footmen had used to strike him on the back of the head. Cosette bent down and found his pipe, which fortunately had not been lit when it fell into the hay. She handed it to him with a grin.

"Jacques, you must sit inside the coach and rest," said Gyles, clapping a hand on the injured coachman's shoulder. "I will drive."

"You?" The Frenchman was possessive of his team, and he protested the plan initially. But after Louisa offered to sit in the box too and make sure Gyles did nothing ham-handed with the horses—and after Cosette offered to sit in the carriage with him and tend his throbbing head—he agreed to the matter and climbed weakly into the carriage.

Gyles helped Louisa up into the box and then carefully guided the carriage out into the darkened stable yard. "We mustn't forget your trunk," he said. Slowly, he guided the carriage towards the gravel path where he had left the trunk in the garden.

"Who is that?" demanded Louisa, grabbing Gyles' arm in alarm.

By the light of the moon, they could make out a tall, slender shape staring down at the trunk. Was it another of the Empress' footmen, sent to accost them and prevent their departure? The man looked up as the coach approached. He was making out their faces by the dim light from the carriage lanterns.

"I say, Lady Lou! What are you doing here in France?"

"Oh, Mr. Smythe," said Louisa, her voice filled with relief. "I might ask the same of you."

Gyles hopped down from the carriage box and bent over to retrieve it.

"Is thish your trunk?" the blond Englishman asked in bewilderment. "And is thish...Mr. Audeley!" He sounded as if he had imbibed more of Empress Josephine's rum punch than he ought and was now wandering the grounds to clear his head. But by the keen way he was eyeing them, Gyles began to wonder if Mr. Smythe's penchant for drinking was more show than actuality.

"Hello again," said Gyles, shifting the trunk to balance it on his left shoulder and reaching out to shake Horatio Smythe's hand. The firm grip Mr. Smythe gave him was quite noticeable until it relaxed into the flaccid floppiness more typical of the inebriated. "I hope you're taking eggshellent care of her." He met Gyles' eye.

"Indeed," said Gyles. "We're leaving France as soon as possible."

Mr. Smythe released his hand and reached into his waistcoat pocket. "Here." he said in low tones. "This might help." He handed Gyles a folded paper which Gyles palmed and then slipped into his own pocket.

"Good-bye, Mr. Smythe," said Louisa as Gyles secured the trunk to the back of the carriage.

"Good-bye, Lady Lou," replied Mr. Smythe, waving his hand—as incongruous a figure in the grounds of Malmaison as the ostrich or the kangaroo. The carriage pulled away until his shadowy silhouette disappeared in the blackness.

"He recognized both of us right away," said Louisa. "What do you think he is doing in France? He's just the sort of muddle-head I would expect Josephine to collect, but I wouldn't think he would have braved the Channel crossing or the blockade just to come to a house party."

"I'm not positive," said Gyles, who had been turning the same question over in his mind, "but the last time I saw him, he said something about diplomatic service for the Crown. With Prince George about to assume the Regency, the war with Napoleon may become more fierce. And the Crown may want to know just how loyal Josephine remains to Napoleon after the divorce."

Louisa's large eyes grew even wider. "A spy? You're saying that Mr. Horatio Smythe is a spy?"

"Are you sorry now you didn't accept him?" Gyles nudged her with his elbow. "He would have made a much more glamorous husband than I."

"Of course not. And such speculation is utterly ridiculous. If he *were* an agent of the Crown, the empress would have ferreted out his purposes before he could say boo."

"Maybe," said Gyles thoughtfully. "But I'm beginning to think he's far cleverer than he lets on."

"Hmm," said Louisa, not quite ready to believe him on that topic.

They continued through the park until they came to the main road. "Are you sorry?" asked Louisa suddenly. "That you did not get to explore the empress' greenhouse in full? And that you did not get to take cuttings back with you for your own garden?"

Gyles, concentrating on keeping the horses out of the hedgerows on this moonless night, took a moment to answer her. "How could I be sorry? I have a lifetime to gather a garden like hers, but some things come into one's life only once."

"Or twice," murmured Louisa.

"Or twice," repeated Gyles, laughing in agreement. He would always be grateful that the girl from the Carlton House gardens had reappeared in his life a second time.

Ahead of them, the road forked, one side heading west towards Paris, the other side heading north to Picardy. "Where to now?" Louisa asked. "It would be the height of folly to return to Paris with Alphonse in such a temper and Empress Josephine set against us."

"But what about your mother's jewels?" Gyles had assumed they must, at least, stop by Paris briefly to retrieve the rest of his beloved's belongings.

"I am not sentimental. If you can afford to lose the world's greatest collection of rosarian knowledge, I can afford to lose a few necklaces. And besides, if we need travel expenses, I've sewn some sapphires into the hem of this dress. Finding a ship will be the hard part. If Morlaix is the only port sending vessels to England, I daresay we'll have to go west and skirt Paris as best we can—"

"Perhaps, said Gyles, disliking the idea of travelling across the breadth of France without the proper papers. He flicked the reins to encourage the horses on to greater speed. "What does the note in my pocket say?"

"Pardon?" asked Louisa, confused by such a request. After a little further explanation, however, she reached into Gyles waistcoat pocket and found the folded paper from Mr. Smythe. Her eyes strained to read the small script by the light of the moving carriage lantern. "Gyles!" she exclaimed. "There's a boat waiting off the coast of Calais. An English one. And this letter instructs the captain to carry the bearers of this letter over to Dover without delay."

"Well, well," said Gyles. "Apparently, Mr. Smythe *is* more highly connected than one would surmise. North it is! And God willing, we'll be at home in Derbyshire before the week is out."

Epilogue

THE ROAD THROUGH DERBYSHIRE was just as Gyles remembered it, and the lane from Upper Cross to the Audeleys' country house felt as familiar as well-worn buckskins. Louisa had never seen his little corner of England, and he spent the last part of the drive showing her the landmarks, from their neighbour Miss Morrison's farmhouse to the boundary stone that marked his own land.

Cosette and Jacques were no longer with them. Jacques had been loath to leave his carriage and horses behind and Cosette, as it turned out, had been loath to leave Jacques. In recognition of services rendered, Louisa had offered Cosette all the dresses and jewels left behind in Paris. The unlikely pair had departed from Calais to go south again while Gyles and Louisa searched for the sheltered inlet on the east side of Calais. The boat in Mr. Smythe's letter could be characterised as nothing other than a smuggler's vessel that owed a favour to the Crown. The bearded captain took them aboard without question, and the crossing to Dover took less time than a tour of the Empress Josephine's greenhouse.

When they had arrived in Dover, Gyles insisted on calling at a bank to withdraw his own funds instead of visiting a pawn shop with Louisa's sapphires. "I may not be a duke, but I'm not exactly a pauper," he had assured her. With guineas in his pocket, he had secured a coach from the livery stable for himself and his *sister*, as Louisa's reputation would suffer if anyone recognised her name.

From Dover to Derbyshire was the most insufferable part of the trip. Gyles was possessed with a longing to be home, and an even greater longing to have Louisa presiding over his home as mistress of it now and always. He had never struggled to play the gentleman while in the presence of a lady, but being alone with Louisa in a closed carriage for three days was more temptation than he had bargained for, and he had been hard pressed to maintain his reputation as a *preux chevalier*. Finally, as the coachman pulled to a stop in front of the door, he leaped from the carriage door without even bothering to use the step. The February wind whipped at his coat and ruffled his chestnut hair as he helped Louisa disembark.

"Ah, Archie," he said, seeing the butler's nephew goggling at him from behind the open front door. "Can you tell my mother that I'm home?"

"Mrs. Audeley?" asked the silly gudgeon.

"Of course, Mrs. Audeley," said Gyles, tucking Louisa's arm under his as he led her up the stone staircase and into the house.

"Oh, but Mr. Audeley, beggin' yer pardon, she isn't here anymore, and she isn't Mrs. Audeley neither."

"Why, what do you mean?" asked Gyles, shutting the front door that Archie had left open as Louisa began to remove her bonnet and her gloves.

"I believe he means that your mother is now Lady Kendall," said Louisa perceptively, and Archie, overcome with the visitor's golden-haired beauty, could only stare open-mouthed and nod like a stippled brook trout.

Startled, Gyles looked from Archie to Louisa and back again. "Well, then, I suppose there will be less confusion about the place, for I must present to you the soon-to-be new Mrs. Audeley." His face took on a worried look. "But Louisa, I don't know what we shall do without a chaperone until the banns—"

"Congratulations," said a world-weary voice, and the sound of one pair of hands clapping filled the hallway. Gyles wheeled about swiftly to see a tall, brown-haired man, with wide shoulders and handsome jaw, applauding their announcement from the door of the parlour.

"Warrenton!" he uttered with surprise.

"Uncle Nigel!" echoed Louisa, and for the first time in a long while, Gyles heard the sound of fear shimmering in her voice.

—⁓—

"What are you doing here?" demanded Louisa. Her arm tightened around Gyle's firm forearm.

He cannot take you away. He cannot. Gyles will do something about it and stop him.

"That," said the Duke of Warrenton, "is a long story. Perhaps we should sit down in the parlour so I can explain?"

Warily, Louisa walked into the parlour with Gyles and sat down next to him on the sofa. His large, calloused hand covered hers and pressed it gently.

Why are you so frightened? Gyles will take care of you as he always does.

Uncle Nigel sat across from them on an old armchair. A black and white cat came over from its place by the window and leaped up onto his lap. The duke's hand began to stroke it gently, his thumb rubbing a circle just between the ears. He looked strangely at home in the armchair, at home and yet adrift.

"When you disappeared from London, I came looking for you, Louisa—in the company of Lord Kendall and Mrs. Audeley. We thought you were bound for the border at first, thanks to the direction set by the Audeley coach." He nodded to Gyles, a compliment to the diversion that he had orchestrated. "But the trail actually led to Derbyshire, and to this house in particular." The cat adjusted its position on his lap, and the duke adjusted his own position in the chair to accommodate the feline's desire to stretch out fully.

"Imagine your mother's surprise when only her coachman was here with an empty carriage, and the both of you had disappeared without a trace."

Gyles' jaw set like concrete. "A regrettable but unavoidable result in keeping Lady Louisa safe from *you.*"

"I don't deny that I'm to blame in this," said Uncle Nigel, and Louisa was surprised to see him take a conciliatory and even penitent tone. "In fact, if I'd never bargained with Digby, then Louisa would never have run away."

"There would have been no need! But your own greed wouldn't allow me to make a match of my own. It had to be someone of your own choosing who would pay you hand-somely for the opportunity."

Again, Uncle Nigel did not disagree. "And how well I have been served for that selfishness. You see, Louisa, I've been forced to run away from London as well. I took an advance from Digby, and I spent it on all the fripperies I used to love so well. And now I can't show my face until I've paid that debt back—or my face will never look the same again."

Louisa wrinkled her nose. No wonder her uncle had been so adamant that she accept Solomon Digby's advances. He was under the thumb of a moneyed ruffian, and Digby was not above employing physical violence to get what he wanted.

"You seem...different," she said. And he did. The rakish Uncle Nigel of the last two years had almost disappeared. He was more like the kindly Uncle Nigel she remembered from childhood, playing spillikins and riddles with her at Christmas when her parents had forgotten that she existed.

"Do I?" His face was drawn, worn, pale. "I've had a dis-appointment of sorts—no, nothing to do with the money. Something else." The circles he was rubbing on the cat's fur became more agitated.

"So, you won't try to marry me off to Digby any longer?"

"No, no, that's all over. I'm sorry I made that arrangement in the first place."

A wave of relief came over Louisa, and the tension in her shoulders dissipated like steam from a kettle. She had been bearing up under that awful arrangement for so long that she did not even remember what it felt like to have the burden lifted.

"And you'll give your consent to *me* marrying your niece?" interjected Gyles.

Louisa lifted her eyebrows with eager anticipation. If her guardian would comply, she and Gyles could be married in three short weeks instead of waiting almost three months for the happy day.

"Yes, I don't see why I shouldn't." The duke looked at Gyles consideringly. "Your mother's become a friend of mine, you know—that's why she let me take refuge here—you have her eyes, and something of her generosity, I expect."

"I would be quite happy to let you live here for three more weeks," said Gyles with a smile, "so that you can serve as our chaperone before the wedding. But then it's back to London for you, for I shall want my house, and my rose garden, and my wife all to myself."

"Of course," said the duke sensibly. "I've been considering where I shall go next. Not London, but to my estate...or what's left of it. I need to make things right. Or at least, as right as I can make them."

Overjoyed to see the solution to all their difficulties, Louisa rose from the couch and ran forward to take her uncle's hand in her own. "Thank you," she said. "I don't know how much of a compliment this is, but I think, in time, you'll be a better duke than any of the Lymingtons ever have been."

"A low bar indeed," agreed her uncle, "but I shall strive to meet it."

The gentlemen stood up from their seats, and the black and white cat leaped off the duke's shifting lap to take refuge in the cushioned window seat across the room.

"I know that cat," said Gyles speculatively. "It belongs to my neighbour, Miss Morrison. She'll probably come by the house looking for it."

"Yes, you're right. She did come by the house looking for it. More than once. But she's stopped coming by now." The Duke of Warrenton sighed. "And therein lies my disappointment...."

FINIS

Author's Note

I hope you have enjoyed *The Paris Footman*. This is the eleventh Regency I have written, but it surprised me by being the most challenging one of the bunch. I had to align the events of the first half of the book with the events in the earlier *Kendall House* book, *The London Rose* (and make sure there were no contradictions). I also had to do a good deal more research than usual since the latter third of the book is spent in France.

Research, though sometimes laborious, is often a labour of love, and I loved learning more about France during the early 1800s. Paris, in the Napoleonic period, was a time of rebirth after the atrocities of the French Revolution. A new aristocratic class was forming, with Alphonse Aubert being a fictional example of former aristocracy now re-ennobled by Napoleon. The city itself was full of building projects like Napoleon's *Arc de Triomphe*, literary and political salons were attracting the intelligentsia of the day, and French fashion continued to set the tone for all of Europe.

In the timeline of my story, Napoleon's divorce of Josephine in January of 1810 was still a fresh wound. His decision to divorce her was based partially on her infidelities and partially on his need for an heir. He continued to visit her after the divorce and her name was the last word on his lips when he died.

After the divorce, Josephine was allowed to keep Malmaison, a chateau outside Paris that she had spent a fortune remodelling. Her menagerie at Malmaison was famous, consisting of many animals from Australia and Africa. The zebra, kangaroo, chamois, emu, and ostrich mentioned in my story are all animals that she kept at Malmaison at one point or another.

Josephine's greenhouse and plant collection was even more impressive than the animal menagerie. She constructed the largest glass greenhouse in the world at that time and gathered the most varieties of roses. She commissioned an artist, Pierre-Joseph Redouté, to create paintings of the plants, and his paintings are the most famous botanical illustrations from the period. She kept her own notes about different rose cultivars and was an authority on the subject.

Although there are many portraits of Josephine, a few of which I saw in person at the Duke of Wellington's Apsley House last summer, none of them ever show her teeth. She reputedly never revealed her teeth when she smiled. One theory about this is that her teeth were black and decayed, causing her to hide them as much as possible.

Josephine grew up on a sugar plantation on Martinique. One interesting fact is that her given name was actually Marie Josèphe Rose Tascher de La Pagerie. No one called her Josephine until Napoleon began using the name. And apparently, Napoleon's preferences outweighed everything else, for that is the name she is known by in history.

What name did she go by in her younger years?
Her family called her Rose.

—ᥱᥣᥱ—

Thank you for reading *The Paris Footman.* I hope you enjoyed Gyles and Louisa's unlikely romance as a gardener-turned-footman shows a runaway heiress that at least one man in her life is worthy of trust. The next instalment of the *Kendall House Regency Romances* will be *The Derbyshire Dance.*

Book Description:

Nigel Lymington, the new Duke of Warrenton, always played second fiddle to his elder brother's wild exploits. After rising to the title himself, he tries to live up to his family's rakish reputation, only to discover that he has neither the temperament nor the money to indulge in the wastrel Warrenton way of life.

While rusticating in Derbyshire, he encounters a gentlewoman named Miss Belinda Morrison who cares more about tenants and crop rotation than tittle-tattle and court connections. Can Nigel learn to plough a straight enough furrow to attract an honest woman of intelligence and industry? And will Bel Morrison set down her ledgers long enough to let him dance his way into her heart?

An homage to the beloved Georgette Heyer, this clean and wholesome Regency romance follows the adventures of a desperate duke, a competent gentlewoman, a bumbling valet, a scheming baroness, and an intrepid feline.

The Derbyshire Dance will release in Autumn 2025.

Books

by Rosanne E. Lortz

Pevensey Mysteries
To Wed an Heiress
The Duke's Last Hunt
A Duel for Christmas

Allen Abbey Romances
The Gentleman in the Ash Tree
The Lady in the Moneylender's Parlour
The Vicar and the Village Scandal

Kendall House Regency Romances
The London Rose
The Paris Footman

Comfort Quartet
A Brother's Wager
Sketches by the Serpentine